MW00680332

THE
PHANTOM PATROL

SELECTED FICTION WORKS BY
L. RON HUBBARD

FANTASY
The Case of the Friendly Corpse
Death's Deputy
Fear
The Ghoul
The Indigestible Triton
Slaves of Sleep & The Masters of Sleep
Typewriter in the Sky
The Ultimate Adventure

SCIENCE FICTION
Battlefield Earth
The Conquest of Space
The End Is Not Yet
Final Blackout
The Kilkenny Cats
The Kingslayer
The Mission Earth Dekalogy*
Ole Doc Methuselah
To the Stars

ADVENTURE
The Hell Job series

WESTERN
Buckskin Brigades
Empty Saddles
Guns of Mark Jardine
Hot Lead Payoff

A full list of L. Ron Hubbard's
novellas and short stories is provided at the back.

*Dekalogy—a group of ten volumes

L. RON HUBBARD

THE
PHANTOM
PATROL

GALAXY
PRESS

Published by
Galaxy Press, LLC
7051 Hollywood Boulevard, Suite 200
Hollywood, CA 90028

© 2008 L. Ron Hubbard Library. All Rights Reserved.

Any unauthorized copying, translation, duplication, importation or distribution,
in whole or in part, by any means, including electronic copying, storage or
transmission, is a violation of applicable laws.

Mission Earth is a trademark owned by L. Ron Hubbard Library and is used with
permission. *Battlefield Earth* is a trademark owned by Author Services, Inc. and is
used with permission.

Horsemen illustration from *Western Story Magazine* is © and ™
Condé Nast Publications and is used with their permission. Fantasy, Far-Flung
Adventure and Science Fiction illustrations: *Unknown* and *Astounding Science Fiction*
copyright © by Street & Smith Publications, Inc. Reprinted with permission of Penny
Publications, LLC. Cover art: © 1935 Metropolitan Magazines, Inc. Reprinted with
permission of Hachette Filipacchi Media. Story Preview illustration: *Argosy
Magazine* is © 1936 Argosy Communications, Inc. All Rights Reserved.
Reprinted with permission from Argosy Communications, Inc.

Printed in the United States of America.

ISBN-10 1-59212-327-9
ISBN-13 978-1-59212-327-8

Library of Congress Control Number: 2007927635

CONTENTS

STORIES FROM PULP FICTION'S GOLDEN AGE

A ND it *was* a golden age.

The 1930s and 1940s were a vibrant, seminal time for a gigantic audience of eager readers, probably the largest per capita audience of readers in American history. The magazine racks were chock-full of publications with ragged trims, garish cover art, cheap brown pulp paper, low cover prices—and the most excitement you could hold in your hands.

"Pulp" magazines, named for their rough-cut, pulpwood paper, were a vehicle for more amazing tales than Scheherazade could have told in a million and one nights. Set apart from higher-class "slick" magazines, printed on fancy glossy paper with quality artwork and superior production values, the pulps were for the "rest of us," adventure story after adventure story for people who liked to *read*. Pulp fiction authors were no-holds-barred entertainers—real storytellers. They were more interested in a thrilling plot twist, a horrific villain or a white-knuckle adventure than they were in lavish prose or convoluted metaphors.

The sheer volume of tales released during this wondrous golden age remains unmatched in any other period of literary history—hundreds of thousands of published stories in over nine hundred different magazines. Some titles lasted only an issue or two; many magazines succumbed to paper shortages during World War II, while others endured for decades yet. Pulp fiction remains as a treasure trove of stories you can read, stories you can love, stories you can remember. The stories were driven by plot and character, with grand heroes, terrible villains, beautiful damsels (often in distress), diabolical plots, amazing places, breathless romances. The readers wanted to be taken beyond the mundane, to live adventures far removed from their ordinary lives—and the pulps rarely failed to deliver.

In that regard, pulp fiction stands in the tradition of all memorable literature. For as history has shown, good stories are much more than fancy prose. William Shakespeare, Charles Dickens, Jules Verne, Alexandre Dumas—many of the greatest literary figures wrote their fiction for the readers, not simply literary colleagues and academic admirers. And writers for pulp magazines were no exception. These publications reached an audience that dwarfed the circulations of today's short story magazines. Issues of the pulps were scooped up and read by over thirty million avid readers each month.

Because pulp fiction writers were often paid no more than a cent a word, they had to become prolific or starve. They also had to write aggressively. As Richard Kyle, publisher and editor of *Argosy*, the first and most long-lived of the pulps, so pointedly explained: "The pulp magazine writers, the best of them, worked for markets that did not write for critics or attempt to satisfy timid advertisers. Not having to answer to anyone other than their readers, they wrote about human beings on the edges of the unknown, in those new lands the future would explore. They wrote for what we would become, not for what we had already been."

Some of the more lasting names that graced the pulps include H. P. Lovecraft, Edgar Rice Burroughs, Robert E. Howard, Max Brand, Louis L'Amour, Elmore Leonard, Dashiell Hammett, Raymond Chandler, Erle Stanley Gardner, John D. MacDonald, Ray Bradbury, Isaac Asimov, Robert Heinlein—and, of course, L. Ron Hubbard.

In a word, he was among the most prolific and popular writers of the era. He was also the most enduring—hence this series—and certainly among the most legendary. It all began only months after he first tried his hand at fiction, with L. Ron Hubbard tales appearing in *Thrilling Adventures, Argosy, Five-Novels Monthly, Detective Fiction Weekly, Top-Notch, Texas Ranger, War Birds, Western Stories,* even *Romantic Range.* He could write on any subject, in any genre, from jungle explorers to deep-sea divers, from G-men and gangsters, cowboys and flying aces to mountain climbers, hard-boiled detectives and spies. But he really began to shine when he turned his talent to science fiction and fantasy of which he authored nearly fifty novels or novelettes to forever change the shape of those genres.

Following in the tradition of such famed authors as Herman Melville, Mark Twain, Jack London and Ernest Hemingway, Ron Hubbard actually lived adventures that his own characters would have admired—as an ethnologist among primitive tribes, as prospector and engineer in hostile climes, as a captain of vessels on four oceans. He even wrote a series of articles for *Argosy,* called "Hell Job," in which he lived and told of the most dangerous professions a man could put his hand to.

Finally, and just for good measure, he was also an accomplished photographer, artist, filmmaker, musician and educator. But he was first and foremost a *writer,* and that's the L. Ron Hubbard we come to know through the pages of this volume.

This library of Stories from the Golden Age presents the best of L. Ron Hubbard's fiction from the heyday of storytelling, the Golden Age of the pulp magazines. In these eighty volumes, readers are treated to a full banquet of 153 stories, a kaleidoscope of tales representing every imaginable genre: science fiction, fantasy, western, mystery, thriller, horror, even romance—action of all kinds and in all places.

Because the pulps themselves were printed on such inexpensive paper with high acid content, issues were not meant to endure. As the years go by, the original issues of every pulp from *Argosy* through *Zeppelin Stories* continue crumbling into brittle, brown dust. This library preserves the L. Ron Hubbard tales from that era, presented with a distinctive look that brings back the nostalgic flavor of those times.

L. Ron Hubbard's Stories from the Golden Age has something for every taste, every reader. These tales will return you to a time when fiction was good clean entertainment and the most fun a kid could have on a rainy afternoon or the best thing an adult could enjoy after a long day at work.

Pick up a volume, and remember what reading is supposed to be all about. Remember curling up with a *great story.*

—Kevin J. Anderson

KEVIN J. ANDERSON *is the author of more than ninety critically acclaimed works of speculative fiction, including* The Saga of Seven Suns, *the continuation of the Dune Chronicles with Brian Herbert, and his* New York Times *bestselling novelization of L. Ron Hubbard's* Ai! Pedrito!

THE
PHANTOM PATROL

CHAPTER ONE

THE SINKING PLANE

CRISP and brittle, the staccato torrent ripped out from the headphones. "SOS . . . SOS . . . Down in storm twenty miles south of Errol Island. SOS . . . Hull leaking. Starboard wing smashed . . . Cannot last two hours . . . SOS . . . Transport Plane New Orleans-bound sinking twenty miles—"

Johnny Trescott's opinion of the matter was amply summed up in a single word, "Damn!"

"Bad news, Chief?" asked Heinie Swartz, above the yelling gale.

"We've got to forget Georges Coquelin," Johnny replied. "This makes the third time in a row. Why can't these Two-Continents pilots take care of themselves?"

Heinie Swartz eyed the dripping foredeck of the lunging seventy-five-footer. Green seas topped with froth were breaking. The one-pound gun was alternately swallowed and disgorged by water. The two 200-hp Sterling Diesels throbbed under the deck, pounding out their hearts against the blow. For five hours the Coast Guard patrol boat 1004 had barely held her own.

Heinie turned back to Trescott, noting the wild look in the CPO's sea blue eyes. "Don't take it so tough, Johnny. Georges will still be around."

"Sure," muttered Johnny. "Sure. But he's getting into my curly locks, even so. He'll run a hundred thousand dollars' worth of dope into the coast tonight, and nobody will be there to say boo! Hell, this will make the third time!"

Heinie eyed the earphones, which still crackled stridently. "Well, you can't leave that crate to sink."

"No, we can't leave it to sink," Johnny agreed. He turned to the helmsman standing two feet behind him. "Change your course to south-southwest."

The helmsman stared from under the damp, glistening brim of his sou'wester. "But, Johnny! That'll stick us into the trough! It'll knock the stuffing—"

"I said change the course," Johnny rapped. "Who the hell is captain of this scow, anyway?"

Heinie thrust his head out of the doorway and brought it back in an instant, drenched. "Blow's picking up. Be a hurricane before morning. Never did like this coast off here anyway. Give me N'Yawk every time. I was telling Max yesterday that this Louisiana duty was the bunk. All sweat and no time in port. If it keeps up—"

"Shut up," said Johnny, "they're calling again." He slapped the phones back over the sides of his damp head.

"SOS . . . SOS . . . Transport Plane 37 in sinking condition twenty miles south of Errol Island . . . Hull filling with water . . . Two pilots, James Ferguson and hostess aboard . . . SOS—"

Johnny Trescott picked up his key. Bracing himself against the dripping side of the pilothouse, he rattled, "Coast Guard patrol boat 1004 on its way. Keep your belt buckled."

"Okay," clicked the receiver. "Okay, Coast Guard."

Johnny hung the phones over a peg. "Good boys, those Two-Continents pilots. Cool as a ton of ice."

"Don't talk about ice," complained Heinie, "I'm out on my feet for a drink. Who's aboard her?"

"The pilots, the hostess and one passenger. Bird by the name of James Ferguson. I'll bet he's having a tough time of it."

"James Ferguson? Of New Orleans? Why," said Heinie, "he's the guy with all the dough. Made it in real estate. Hostess too, huh? That's good news. They're generally swell girls."

Johnny growled, "Nix on that dope. This isn't New York."

The CG-1004 was now in the trough. The great green mountains hit her broadside, smothered her, but each time she went down she struggled back, shaking herself like a gray whippet. Occasionally she ran against a cross wave. The effect was the same as a train striking a mountainside. She crashed down, stayed there for a moment, shuddering, and then, as if the effort was far too great, came sluggishly back, to plow onward again. The deckhouse windows were alternately green with sea and gray with sky.

Johnny Trescott pulled the bill of his battered white-topped cap down over his left eye and sighed. "Would have been all set if this hadn't come up!"

"Oh, stop worrying about Georges. He'll still be around. What's it to you anyway?"

"Plenty. I've been chasing him all over the Gulf of Mexico for two months. He's landed enough dope to supply the US for years to come."

"I don't like those dope guys. The rummies, now," said

5

Heinie, judicially, "they were different. They knew they weren't going to get anything stiff and they never did a thing about it. But dope— I remember one guy we nailed off Maine. Had a three-inch gun and three machine guns. That was one sweet fight. Means a lot of time to those birds if they're caught."

Johnny nodded. "They're poison, Heinie. But this Georges makes the rest of them look sick. He's got a couple murders tied to his tail already."

"What's he look like?"

"Nobody knows. Runs a fast twin-Diesel ship with about thirty men aboard."

"And we were going to tackle her with this scow?" Heinie whistled.

"Sure. Orders are orders, aren't they? I hope he didn't get that radio. Ferguson would be good bait to bring him around. We'd have a hard time fighting him and taking that plane out of the water, too."

The earphones were chattering crisply once more. "Sinking fast. This is last message. The others are on the top wing. Ferguson is offering ten thousand to you if you get here in time."

Johnny threw the switch. His finger quivered on the key. "Hold everything. We'll be with you in twenty minutes. Can you hold out?"

"Okay, Coast Guard. Okay. I'm going up to admire the view."

"She's in a bad way," said Johnny. He leaned over the engine room tube. "Hi! Joe! Get a little more out of those tin cans, will you?"

6

Blasphemy sizzled back up the brass cylinder. "What the hell do you think this is, anyway? I'm ripping hell out of her as it is!"

"That's your worry, not mine," barked Johnny. "He's sore," he told Heinie. "Must be a hundred and twenty down there."

"Think we'll make it?"

Johnny shrugged. "Might bust down before we even get near to it. Hope that Georges doesn't pick this up and come tailing up. That would be bad."

"Think he would?"

"If you'd chased that guy as long as I have, Heinie, you'd know all about him. You're damned right he would. And plenty more." Johnny looked into the spinning compass bowl. "You're a point off your course, sailor."

"She's bucking," protested the helmsman.

"Well, did you think she'd pray? Lean into it, you dummy! We've got fifteen minutes left to get there. Otherwise, all we'll find will be a couple struts."

Under the additional two knots, the patrol boat was straining every timber in her sleek hull. The waves were sledgehammers, and the sea and sky spun like a jumpy motion picture. The muzzle of the one-pounder drooled saltwater. Its plug had long since been snatched away.

Except for the translucent side walls of the house-sized waves, the sea was the color of the sky. The horizon itself was obscured, but heaven and water touched, seemingly, a hundred yards before the bow.

"It's getting thick," observed Heinie. "Be the devil finding the plane, even if we almost run it down."

"You'll have to stick your nose out there and smell it," Johnny grinned.

"Say, lay off my nose. I can't be a collar ad like you."

Johnny grinned, more to hide the worry which seeped into his eyes than to stamp Heinie as a humorist. The wind-whipped leather of his face was taut. His hard jaw pulsated. Johnny knew they might run within a thousand yards of the plane and miss it altogether.

He looked back at the lashing thread of the log. The spinning propeller of the knotage instrument was at times entirely out of the water. Small chance to trust that thing. But the dripping dial and the ticking chronometer said that they were less than a mile away from the shattered transport plane. Four people, drenched and weary, and clinging to a wing . . .

"Hope Georges didn't beat us to it," murmured Johnny. "Glue your ugly pan to that port, Heinie, and look sharp. We'll be there in a moment."

Johnny tugged at his cap and tried to appear at ease. Long and rangy, he leaned against the chart table and looked ahead. He had a dread of the floating things which had been men. Too many of them in this work.

"What's that two points off the port bow?" he said.

"Dunno. Can't see it."

"Looks like a—by golly, I'll bet it is. Sheer off!" he cried to the helmsman. "And don't flop us over!"

"It's a wing," replied Heinie, squinting his watery eyes. "They're right close to us."

"Wouldn't kid me, would you? There they are, Heinie.

That's the girl on this side. Poor kid looks like she's all worn out."

"The hell she is!" cried Heinie. "She's holding that fat guy from sliding off. Look at her wave!"

Johnny turned to the brass speaking tube. "Slack off, Joe—we've arrived!"

CHAPTER TWO

THE ATTACK

JOHNNY TRESCOTT took a megaphone and went out of the deckhouse. A wave catapulted at him, frothing, green, swirling. He caught a lifeline and held on through the smother of saltwater. Disgorged, he waved the megaphone at the battered plane. The girl on the end waved back.

A sailor brought up a coil of light line with a monkey fist attached. He swung it around his head and shot it toward the wing.

"Make it fast!" bellowed Johnny through the megaphone.

A slim youngster, his gold-braided coat flapping in the wind, scooped up the line and tied it around an aileron post. Johnny fastened a heavier line to the first and then bawled, "Haul in!"

The youngster beckoned to the girl that she would be first. But she shook her head and passed the fat man down the wing. The fat man lifted a blanched face at the patrol boat and then grabbed at the line.

"Duck him good!" shouted Heinie at Johnny's elbow. "He's yellow. That's Ferguson!"

There was little need to pay heed to Heinie's order. Ferguson slid off the wing, arms flailing. He hit the center of a wave, to be instantly swallowed up. He clawed the water, shrieking. Johnny braced his feet and, through the smother of green

11

sea, hauled in on the line. Bringing Ferguson into the lee, he pulled him up.

"Thank God!" cried Ferguson. "Thank God! Thank God! Thank God!"

"Take him below," shouted Johnny at a sailor, and Ferguson went, scrambling for a footing on the wave-hammered deck. Heinie looked after him disgustedly.

The youngster was pulling the heavy line back to the plane. It was caught in the waves. It tossed and lashed, bowed by the wind. This time, the girl allowed herself to be encoiled by the rope. She went off the wing in a clean dive, swimming five feet below the surface. Johnny swiftly took up the slack in the line.

"That takes guts!" Johnny shouted to Heinie.

"Ladies don't have guts," Heinie retorted.

Johnny reached down for a slim hand and pulled the girl to the deck. He set her on her feet and then stood staring at her. Abruptly he forgot about the storm, forgot about the plane, forgot everything but the girl. Even the sea water had not marred her beauty. Her face was a delicate cameo done in ivory and topped by a glorious tumble of amber red hair.

"Wake up!" bawled Heinie, grabbing the megaphone. "Haul in!" he shouted at the plane.

The girl wiped the water out of her eyes and smiled. "Thanks, sailor."

"Okay," said Johnny, recovering his voice. "I'm Johnny Trescott. Who are you?"

She smiled, laughter brimming into her ultramarine eyes. "Alicia Reynolds, Mr. Trescott. If you—"

A mountain range, green and frothy, slashed at them, buried them. Johnny caught at her waist and held to the lifeline. When the water was gone, she threw her hair out of her eyes and then reached down to give a hand to the youngster who was being hauled in.

"Go aft," ordered Johnny, a little brusque.

Unperturbed, she said, "All right, Billie?"

"Get that rope back," said the youngster she had called Billie. "Mac says she's about to go under."

The elder of the two pilots was bracing himself with one foot against the gas tank cap on top of the wing. Hand over hand, calmly avoiding the fouling of the line, the pilot called Mac brought the heavy rope up and wound it about his waist. He plunged over the side and came up spluttering. With a clumsy breast stroke he struck out for the patrol boat. Waves boosted him and dropped him twenty feet in the breath of a single, stinging second.

Johnny pulled him up. The girl sighed with relief and then turned to go aft. The pilot called Mac dashed the water from his burning eyes and pointed to the opposite side of the boat.

"Friends of yours?" asked Mac.

Johnny whirled. Through the tumble of water he could see a vague shape drawing abreast of them. It was a black low-lying cruiser of ominous proportions.

"Get below!" rapped Johnny at the two pilots and the girl.

When they had gone, Heinie held on tight and stared at the ship, which was drawing nearer. "Who is it?"

"Three guesses, Heinie. The first three don't count."

"My God, Johnny! You mean that's Georges Coquelin?"

"In person. Run up some shells for the one-pounder and have Haines break out a machine gun. We're going to have a little party."

"But they're too close! They'll blow us out of the—" A towering sea battered Heinie against the side of the deckhouse. He struggled toward the hatch.

Johnny gave the black ship a bitter smile. No one knew better than he that the presence of Georges Coquelin was not a coincidence. That line in the SOS about Ferguson . . . Ferguson could be held for ransom—big ransom.

"Run out the shells!" bawled Johnny after his retreating exec. "We'll hold him as long as we can." He thumped the holstered .45 which banged against his thigh.

The pitching black line cruiser began to slacken speed. Its wake still boiling, it swerved around in a three-hundred-and-sixty-degree turn to come back alongside. A tall blond man was holding the bridge rail with tight fists. Two sailors worked at something shiny behind the wheel. A machine gun.

Johnny lurched toward the deckhouse. Inside he grabbed the brass tube. "Joe! Get going! Georges sneaked up on us. Full speed!"

"Hell!" bellowed Joe, deep in the ship. "We strained a reduction gear while we were laying to!"

"Did you take it apart?"

"Yes."

"Why, of all the—! Okay, Joe. If you don't get it together in five minutes, you won't have any engines to monkey with. Snap into it!"

"Run up some shells for the one-pounder and have Haines break out a machine gun. We're going to have a little party."

Heinie struggled up to the dripping one-pounder with a box of shells which he jammed into the rack. Johnny slued the weapon about.

A smooth voice drifted across the intervening hundred yards. "Lay off that gun, sailor. We want Ferguson."

The megaphone rolled in the scuppers. Johnny snatched it up. "Go to hell!" he shouted.

From the bridge of the pitching black ship came a sound like a thousand hammers beating simultaneously on tin. A window shattered in the deckhouse. Slugs ripped splinters from the planks.

Johnny rammed a shell into the breech. He waited until the patrol boat bucked upward. The lanyard jerked and the gun jumped. Heinie slammed another into the breech.

"Lower!" bawled Heinie. "Hull him! Don't try for the bridge!"

A sailor came up beside Johnny. "I'll take it."

Johnny stepped aside and picked up the megaphone. The machine gun had stopped.

"Coquelin! Shove off, or we'll sink you!"

The tall blond man on the cruiser's bridge threw back his head and laughed. Then he shouted through cupped hands, "Look at my forward deck!"

The black ship was drawing astern of them. The patrol boat was pitching in the trough, hard to hit and harder to shoot from. On the forward deck of the cruiser, a three-inch gun was menacing them. Beside it a one-pounder was a child's plaything.

"Knock the pants off him," begged Heinie. "He's not so tough. We'll run away from him in a minute."

"The hell we will. That dumb son Joe dismantled the reduction gear while we were taking the people off the plane."

The gray sky met the green sea. The waves smashed and roared over the forward deck. The black ship was astern and coming up on the starboard side. The range was less than fifty yards, but a dozen frowning mountain ranges intervened. The blond man on the bridge gripped the rail and leaned forward expectantly. Behind him two men crouched beside the machine gun, waiting for his signal.

Johnny fought his way back to the deckhouse. "Joe!" he shouted into the tube. "Can't you *do* something?"

"In a few minutes, Johnny—"

"Step on it. There aren't many left!"

Back on deck, Johnny heard Coquelin shout, "Lay off that gun or I'll blast you. Hand over Ferguson."

Johnny turned to Heinie. Past Heinie, the sea was waltzing through thirty degrees. The patrol boat's bucking made it hard to stick with her.

"He means it," said Johnny. "It won't be the first time. Hold your fire with that gun, sailor. We couldn't get him the first shot."

"What you going to do," raved Heinie, "stand there and let him take Ferguson? We'd be the laughing stock of the base! For God's sake, Johnny!"

"Shut up. We've got passengers aboard us and I've got to protect them, haven't I?"

17

Georges Coquelin loomed more distinct as the distance lessened between them. He was Johnny's height and had Johnny's blond hair and leathery complexion. "What about it?" He pointed significantly at the three-incher. Sailors were peeling off the canvas lashings and making ready with a shell.

Out of the patrol boat's after hatch, a sailor struggled up with a machine gun.

"Hold that fire!" shouted Johnny.

"We can't fight," Heinie wailed. "The devil's got the drop on us. If we just—" They were buried again in the green swirl. When the wave had gone, the pitching black ship was still there. The wind screamed through the radio mast of the CG-1004.

On the black ship's bow were the words *The Maid from Hell.* The lettering was easily read. The cruiser was drifting in toward them. A grim hulk of a man was dropping fenders over the side to protect the paintwork if they crashed against the patrol boat. The cool assurance of the move was jarring.

Johnny's eyes were the size of pinpoints. Small white fires leaped down in their blue depths. He braced his rangy length against the shock of the waves and went again to the brass speaking tube.

"Joe!"

"Sorry, Johnny. I guess I—"

"Can't you get underway? Even with one engine?"

"No, Johnny. You see, I—"

"Hell!" rapped Johnny and went back to the deck. Men were boiling out of the cruiser's hatches. They held to the railing for support. At their sides guns were tied down tight. Rifles were in their clenched hands. There were fifteen of them.

"They're going to board us," said Johnny. "You take this end of the ship, I'll take the other. When they drop down, let 'em have it."

"Okay," said Heinie, relieved. He hoisted at his holstered pistol.

Johnny fought back to the stern of the patrol boat. The men were ready to drop at the first touch of the ships.

Johnny waved the machine gunner into the protection of a hatch. He himself stood in plain sight, waiting, Colt in hand. Georges Coquelin, high above him, grinned down.

Coquelin drew out his own automatic. "Go easy, sailor," he shouted.

Johnny fought down the impulse to shoot the man. He would gain nothing by that. Coquelin was the only one who could hold his own crew in check. They were vicious devils, that crew. Recruited from all the scum of a dozen ports.

The first one dropped. Johnny watched him hit the deck and grab for handholds. In his wake came the rest, swarming down with clenched fists, beady eyes. Three men lumbered aft toward Johnny. A mighty sea thundered over them and they came out of it gasping. The first hefted his gun, whipping the water from the barrel. The gun roared.

Johnny had ducked. He dived headfirst toward them, into the protection they afforded from Coquelin. The .45 barked. The first man took it just above the belt. A sea carried him, still twitching, over the side. Johnny dived sideways, trying

19

to get far enough back for another shot. From the forward deck he heard the racket of guns.

Six more boarded and joined the three. A human avalanche, they swept down upon Johnny, hands upraised, arms swinging loose and ready. A sea battered them back. Again they came on.

From the deck of *The Maid from Hell,* Georges Coquelin took a careful bead on Johnny. The automatic barked. Johnny reeled. A wave tugged at him. His knees buckled, his hands broke at the wrists. He fell forward, hanging half into the sea, insecurely held by a stanchion. Waves licked at his hair.

CHAPTER THREE

THE PHANTOM STRIKES

THE hurricane season had departed, leaving in its wake the ripped remains of houses and ships. It had sent its ranting storm against the coasts of the Gulf of Mexico, piling the beaches high with floating wreckage. In this wreckage the Coast Guard had delved, wondering, searching for the patrol boat 1004. But nothing was ever found on the strewn sand. No spars, hatches, life belts or planking had been caught and held by the fangs of reefs. The CG-1004 had vanished just as the *Cyclops* had vanished.

The CG-1004 was but a seventy-five-footer, manned by six men, under the command of a CPO. Its disappearance was no great marine tragedy. The news of the loss barely made the shipping news. The CG-1004 was but a relic of the rum-chasing days which would, the Coast Guard prayed, come no more. Even had it survived, it would have been decommissioned.

Besides, the headlines at the time of the patrol boat's disappearance were far too filled with greater news. The loss of Transport Plane 37, of the Two-Continents Airways, sent a ripple of speculation across the breadth of the United States. A ripple of sorrow. Not for the two pilots. Bill Johnson and Mac Craig were missed by their flying brothers only. Nor was the sorrow stretched to include the loss of Alicia Reynolds, the hostess of 37. These mentions were but incidental. Aviation had merely taken another toll of lives, and people shook their heads about it and went out on Sunday to wreck their fine cars and kill themselves on the highways.

But they remembered Ferguson. James George Ferguson. The man who spent millions to make millions, and who coveted a political throne in the sun. The man who had changed swamps to splendid resorts. Ferguson, the idol of the financiers, the brain that juggled stocks with subtle deftness. James G. Ferguson, the wizard of finance, was gone and no one had the courage to take his place.

There were rumors, as there always are, that a ransom had been requested. But undoubtedly this was the work of cranks. Ferguson, of course, was dead in the depths of the sea, victim of flying. James George Ferguson had pulled financial wires for the last time. His round face and bald pink head would be seen no more.

For many weeks no one connected these facts with the Phantom, not even the harassed men at Coast Guard headquarters. The Phantom, that gray, sinister ghost which slid through the fogs on its errands of death, was only a hallucination. Everyone at headquarters, even Admiral Baird in Washington, stated that such a thing was impossible. Captains had looked too long through the impenetrable mists; their judgment was faulty. The Phantom could not be a Coast Guard patrol boat, and it was not. The powers that were so decreed it, but the newspapers had refused to believe. Terror was felt to seep down into the region of Mississippi and Louisiana.

There were passengers who had sworn to the facts, but no one in his right mind would trust the vision of an excited passenger. They had seen the Phantom. It had numbers on its bow and the white letters CG. And the pirates who came looting other ships had been dressed in naval uniforms. The officer in charge wore a shield on his white cap. Assuredly, these marked the Phantom as a Coast Guard patrol boat.

The toll of robbery at sea mounted steadily, certainly. A captain was killed aboard this ship, a mate was shot to death aboard that. Each time, the ship's company swore by all the holy seraphs that the work had been done by a patrol boat.

And then the SS *Marlane* was attacked at her anchorage.

The SS *Marlane* had been waiting for morning and customs officers, and she had swung at her chains out in the stream off New Orleans. At midnight, the fog was split apart with lights and a giant's voice bellowed that the gangway should be lowered, in the name of the United States Coast Guard.

The captain, tired after a long trip, grudgingly obeyed. He saw a tall, blond man swing over the side. A man who wore the uniform of a CPO in the Coast Guard. The man's eyes were blue; his hair was almost white. In the light of the blue deck lantern he appeared young.

At the first hail, a young gentleman came out on deck. A newspaper reporter from the North, a man whose pen dealt with international subjects and was therefore inviolate. He saw the Coast Guard boat and he saw the mysterious blond man. He was lined up against a bulwark while men in blue jumpers went through the strongroom and through the passengers' pockets.

23

They found the captain later, lying in front of the gangway, his head smashed.

The newspaperman wrote the story, as newspapermen will. He told all the details without any flight of imagination. And because he dealt with international affairs, Admiral Baird, up in Washington, believed. There were the facts: A tall, white-headed man with blue eyes, wearing the uniform of the Coast Guard. A seventy-five-foot patrol boat.

Admiral Baird's chief aide went to the files and unearthed there every available item of information that could possibly be brought to bear on the case. And when they went through it all Admiral Baird nodded.

"I understand, now," he boomed. "I understand it all. This young fellow, this John Trescott, what do we know of his past history?"

"Nothing," the aide echoed. "Nothing at all. Because he was proficient in the use of boats and arms, we recruited him when the rummies were driving us hardest. He should have been paid off when his usefulness was ended. According to these letters, he entered the Coast Guard because he was bored, wanted excitement. Because he was young and willing, we made him a chief petty officer."

"Precisely!" the Admiral said. "He entered the Coast Guard for one purpose. Somehow he was connected with a smuggling crew in the Gulf. They needed this boat for various purposes. And he took the opportunity offered him by the storm to disappear with his entire crew. If we find John Trescott, we will find the Phantom, and we can place a stop to these nefarious activities."

It was the aide's turn to nod. "I had not thought of that, but I understand. It is certain that he is the head of this. I will set the traps and we will post a lookout along that coast. We will watch the dives in New Orleans. Admiral, John Trescott will be in our hands this month."

"This month?" boomed the Admiral. "These activities have gone on for three months now. Stop it in a week, understand?" The admiral plucked at the clippings again. Once more his eyes gleamed. "Listen! Transport Plane 37 disappeared that night. James Ferguson was aboard it. John Trescott rescued the plane and kidnaped James Ferguson! Those ransom rumors were true. Release this to the press immediately. Give a general order to all ships and stations. Comb the Gulf!

"Before long, this John Trescott will pay his reckoning. Murder, barratry, desertion, kidnaping for ransom, stopping vessels on the high seas for purposes of robbery."

The aide bobbed his head. Typewriters clattered in the outer office. The general orders were already on the wire. . . .

CHAPTER FOUR

GEORGES COQUELIN

ALONG the horizon, the clouds looked green. Green and purple and red, colors which were mirrored to perfection in the glassy surface of the Gulf. Here and there a great billow reared up like a castle, or a prehistoric animal, or a city. The sun was a red caldron of lava, almost out of sight over the rim.

Alicia Reynolds leaned back in the sand and pointed a slim finger at the sky. Her eyes were laughing. "Look, Johnny, look! There's a plane! See?"

Johnny Trescott started to his feet, staring. "Where?"

"No, no, no. Not a real one, just a cloud. See that tuft of—" She looked at his eyes and found sorrow in the sea blue depths. "I'm sorry, Johnny. Won't you ever believe that it wasn't your fault?"

"When all is right with the world, with you, with the boys, I'll forget about it. Until then, I can't. I know it was me. I'm dumb, Alicia, honest I am. I should have opened up on them and taken the consequences."

"Stop, silly! Your shoulders are broad, but not that big. Georges would have blown us out of the water and we'd all be dead. It's better this way. Things aren't too bad. We've been here only a short time."

"Three months," Johnny told her, grimly.

"That long? You shouldn't keep count, it makes it harder. Things aren't too bad, are they, Johnny?"

"I guess they could be worse. If only Georges would keep his filthy paws away from you!"

"He doesn't dare touch me, Johnny. Not while you're here, he doesn't."

"But how long will I be here? I wonder why he didn't leave me aboard the boat. I wonder why he doesn't kill me some night when I'm asleep. He's had enough chances. Even when I slugged him that time, he didn't shoot me. Just grinned at me and put his gun back. He's a funny lad, that Georges Coquelin."

"There's an answer to everything, if you look long enough for it, Johnny. I'd tell you the answer to this, if it didn't sound so—so—well, conceited."

"Go ahead. I won't accuse you of that."

"You see, Johnny, I think Georges really wants me to marry him. He has some religion down deep in him, and no matter what he's done, it crops out once in a while. He knows what I think of you, you see. And he thinks he has some chance of winning me over if he leaves you alone. One of these days, he'll—I won't say it."

"He'll what?" Johnny insisted.

"He'll decide that he can't take me under any other conditions, and he'll do something terrible to you. Torture you, perhaps, to make me give my consent to marriage. Perhaps that—"

Johnny's eyes were burning with deep, well-fed fires of hate. "Don't worry about that."

Alicia smoothed her powder blue blouse and stood up, brushing away the sand which clung to her. The light was failing.

"What's the matter with you today, Johnny? You seem different, some way. Very different."

Johnny's smile was tight. He glanced over his shoulder at the squalid huts which lay just behind the veil of underbrush and trees. He pointed a brown finger out to the cove.

"See that launch out there? It came in this afternoon, just after the patrol boat left."

Alicia stared at it in sudden comprehension. "You mean you'll try—?"

"I'll try tonight. No more than two of us can get away, and it will have to be you and I. Heinie can take care of himself, so can the others. Old Ferguson wouldn't have nerve enough to try it, and besides, he's done nothing but blubber all day. I went up to see him. When it gets good and dark, you and I will make a try for that launch, and if we get away, we can come back with a patrol boat and wipe this place off the face of the earth."

"But the patrol boat will be coming back in a few minutes," protested Alicia. She tossed her amber red hair out of her eyes and held it at the back of her head. "It went over to the wrecked tanker to refuel for a raid, or whatever they do when they go out."

"We'll have to run a chance on that. Maybe it will come back and then leave again. If it does, we can break through the guard and get into the launch and go."

Alicia's hand shook a little as she laid it on Johnny's tattered shoulder. "But are you all right? Has the wound healed enough for that?"

"I'm okay," Johnny replied. "Don't worry about that. It was only a crease in the first place."

Alicia turned back to the sea. Her finely chiseled features were silhouetted against the last light of sunset. She pointed at the headland. "There comes the patrol boat now. We'll have to wait until it leaves."

Together they walked down the sand to the ramshackle, moss-grown float. Heinie was there, watching the patrol boat come in.

"Georges is coming ashore, I guess," said Heinie. "One of these days I'm going to pop him one, just for the devil of it."

Johnny looked back into the darkness of a hut. A black man squatted there, rifle across his knees—just a pair of eyes rolling white and the glint of the gun breech.

"Some other time," said Johnny. "I've a hunch your friend Bilbo would like nothing better than to shoot you down."

Heinie shrugged. "Well, I've got to talk about something, haven't I? It makes me feel good, just to say it. I wish this island wasn't so doggoned far away from the mainland. I'd swim it one of these nights."

"How about the sharks?" said Alicia.

"Aw, the sharks! Down in Tampa, once, I kicked one in the nose and, by golly, he looked like he was going to cry. A barracuda is the only thing you have to worry about in these waters. They only bite you once, but oh, boy!"

"Georges is coming in," said Johnny in a subdued voice.

Georges Coquelin, dressed in one of Johnny Trescott's uniforms, stepped onto the dock and swaggered toward them. He was thin and blond, and his blue eyes were expressionless blotches against the leather of his face.

"Ah," said Georges Coquelin. "A reception committee all in my honor! Good evening, everyone. And good evening, Miss Reynolds. A fine sunset, a fine sunset."

"Good night for a hanging," said Alicia, simply.

Georges shot his glance at her. His eyes were like two foil points stabbing her. He laughed. "Still the spirited lady, aren't you, my dear?"

"Yes, Mr. Coquelin. If that's what you're fishing for, I'm still a lady. In Vermont, lackeys are intelligent enough to know a lady without asking." She smiled, sweetly enough.

Georges laughed again and looked over Johnny's shoulder to make certain that Bilbo and the gun were there, ready.

"We go out tonight," he said, "for the mainland. And if you should happen to be tiring of this reef, Miss Reynolds, allow me to suggest that you accompany us. We will put in at a small harbor where I know the priest."

"I'm sorry," replied Alicia, lightly, "but it so happens that I have other engagements. Some other time, perhaps."

Johnny smiled and then turned to Georges. "You might take us all across with you. You also might return the 1004 to its base. I'm certain that everyone would appreciate it. We might even fix up a reward for you."

"With a rope, *hein*?" Georges laughed again, his expressionless eyes ugly. "And I suppose you are still asking what I do with your good boat."

"You might at least run your own tin can for a while," said Johnny.

"I might, but I won't. You see, business is very poor these late years, and my cruiser, unhappily, uses up a great deal of fuel. That is not economical in the least. Your boat, now, serves the purpose much better. I am never stopped when I land my shipments. It was a stroke of genius that I commandeered it."

Georges looked toward the underbrush, through which several shacks were barely visible in the faded light. "Henri!" he called.

Presently, a hulk of a man shuffled out to the beach, wiping his mouth with the back of his hand.

"Henri," said Georges Coquelin, "there was a little trouble at the fueling base this afternoon. Nothing very much—just an incident—but I find it necessary to recruit another engineer."

"Huh," grunted Henri. "What happened to old Roderick?"

"A little unpleasantness. He demanded a greater share, and became somewhat insistent about it. I regret that I found it necessary to shoot him dead."

"Roderick put up a fight?" Henri was plainly amazed. "That's the third man you've shot this month, Georges. What's the matter? Can't you get on with the boys, or is it because you want fewer men to divvy up the loot with?"

"Henri," said Georges mildly, "my advice on that score is very much to the point. Another remark of the same character and I am very afraid that you will die. Perhaps not so pleasantly as Roderick did, but you will die, anyway."

"Okay, Georges, okay. But don't get mad. I'm telling you,

Georges"—Henri was obviously trying to win back into good favor—"I tell you, Georges, the rest of the boys are griping about it. Here you have this old fossil Ferguson and you don't do anything to collect the ransom. Nothing at all. That old gent is worth a hundred and fifty thousand, if he's worth a plugged *centavo*. The boys are just talking, that's all. Just talking. There were thirty-two of us to begin with, and now there are only twenty-nine."

"Go right on," said Georges, smiling. "I'm listening."

"Well, you see, it's like this." Beads of sweat began to stand out on Henri's greasy forehead. "You see, somebody said that you were planning to join up with these Coast Guarders—see?—and take the girl and the boat and lam out of here. I'm just telling you, Georges, just telling you about the way things stand. Now listen, Georges, listen. There is no reason for you to get sore. Honest there ain't. These aren't my ideas. They're the boys', see? They're just kind of bored." Henri managed a sickly smile. "Just kind of bored. Having this dame around here don't do 'em any good, you understand?"

"Who," said Georges quietly, "first mentioned the possibility that I was attempting to get rid of the rest of you? Who?"

Sweat dripped down into Henri's eyes, blinding him. His knees quivered. His great hands tugged restlessly at his belt. He stammered, looking back at the ominous silence behind him. Three men had come out to the edge and were silently regarding him.

Georges held up his hand. "All right, Bilbo."

The black man scrambled up. The rifle jumped to his

shoulder. Flame ripped through the dusk. Bilbo sank back on his haunches, grinning. Slowly he levered another cartridge into his rifle and placed it back across his knees.

The man called Henri was spitting blood onto the sand. There was little left of his face, and though his legs still jerked, and his hands clawed the white particles, it was obvious that he was dead.

Alicia stumbled back into Johnny's arms, sobbing. Georges went on down the path and climbed back into the boat. Georges was smiling.

"Have a pleasant time, Miss Reynolds. Perhaps you'll come with me next trip."

The new engineer went down to the boat and rowed Georges back to the CG-1004.

Bilbo sank back on his haunches, grinning.
Slowly he levered another cartridge into his rifle
and placed it back across his knees.

CHAPTER FIVE

ESCAPE

JAMES GEORGE FERGUSON, one-time financier, was now but a mound underneath the ragged blanket. His bald head reflected the rays of the yellow hurricane lantern, and his small eyes were glassy. He knew now, after three months, that a financier without the barricade of a desk is nothing. He had come to envy the youth and vitalness which were Johnny Trescott.

Ferguson stared up at the CPO, uneasy under Johnny's direct gaze. He could read in Johnny's weathered face what Johnny thought of him. The picture, to Ferguson, was neither nice nor obscure—but Johnny was courteous enough.

"Feeling better tonight, Mr. Ferguson?" said Johnny.

"Terrible. These mosquitoes! Trescott, can a man get malaria down here? Can he? My forehead feels hot when I touch it, and I have pains in my stomach. Is that malaria, Trescott?"

Johnny felt of the moist head and found it cool. "I don't think you've got malaria. I hope you've been taking quinine."

"Certainly I have."

Johnny opened the box on the table and found all the capsules there. He had gone to no little trouble getting those from Georges. "I'm afraid you haven't," said Johnny.

"But I hate it. Do I have to take that, Trescott? It burns me when I swallow it."

Johnny shrugged. They were alone in the small hut, but Johnny made the fact positive by glancing around. He stepped close to Ferguson.

"Tonight," Johnny said in a low voice, "I'm going to make a break for it."

"You're *what*?" shouted Ferguson.

"Shut up—I mean pipe down, Mr. Ferguson, they'll hear you. I said I'm going to make a break for it. I can't take you with me."

"But you must. I'll pay you a hundred thou—"

"Wait a minute! This is going to require a lot more than money. You're a sick man."

"No, I'm not."

"But you said you were. I'm going to take Miss Reynolds with me. I can't leave her here, because after I'm gone—well, you understand how it is, Mr. Ferguson. She can run like the devil, and I can depend on her."

"But why not take Mr. Swartz? Won't you need—"

Johnny shook his head. "No. I'm taking Alicia. If we get through, we'll go straight to the Coast Guard station and get another patrol boat. Then we'll come back for you. Understand?"

"Yes, yes. But you've got to take me, Trescott. I'll pay—"

"I'm sorry. I can't. I want to know who I'd better see for you ashore."

"My secretary. Harold Clarke. Tell him that he should give you money, help, anything."

"Can't you send him a note?"

"I haven't any paper and I've no pencil. Just tell him, that will be enough. Are you sure you can't take me?"

"Positive. They'd make certain that they'd catch up with us if I took you. I can't run that risk. Harold Clarke is the man. All right, Mr. Ferguson. I'll tell him, if we make it to shore."

Before Ferguson could protest again, Johnny left.

He strode down to the beach and found Heinie sitting against a tree, looking at the sparkling stars.

"There's Orion," said Heinie when Johnny came up beside him. "I've been trying to get an idea where we are."

"I know pretty close," said Johnny. He lowered his voice. "Alicia and I are going to make a run for it tonight."

Heinie continued to gaze at the sky. "That's okay with me. I hope you make it."

"The launch won't hold but two, and I'm afraid to leave Alicia here any longer. You know how it is, Heinie."

"Sure, I know. But be careful of Bilbo. He's down there by the wharf. He might get you. These stars are pretty bright."

"I've thought of that and I want your help, Heinie. Alicia is on the other side of the wharf, waiting. The men are all up in the main hut getting lit to the gills."

"Maybe you'd better wait until Little Joe comes on. He and I are pretty thick, Johnny. I've been working on him."

"No. We can't wait that long. The patrol boat may come back, and the launch will be gone by dawn. We'll have to risk Bilbo. Come with me, will you?"

Heinie got up and stretched, yawning. Then he followed Johnny down to the boat shed. Johnny was whistling, giving

Bilbo ample warning that they were coming up on him. Bilbo sometimes shot at silent shadows, just in case.

"Stop, white man," said Bilbo in a whiny voice. "Keep away from the float. You ain't never to go down there, unnerstan'?"

"Okay, Bilbo," said Heinie. "I was going up to the huts, anyway. Big party up there tonight."

Bilbo's shrill whine came out of the deep shadow. "Always big party up there. Never see the time there wasn't. Git along, if you're goin'."

Heinie ambled out of sight into the underbrush. Johnny sat on his heels looking at the water. At length, he addressed the man.

"That was pretty good shooting today, Bilbo."

"Pretty good. Never did like that Henri noway. Big mouth, no brains. Tried all day yesterday to get the boys to pull out with him in *The Maid from Hell*. Georges done right by having that Henri shot."

"You like your work, don't you?" said Johnny.

"Sure. Fine work. Nothin' to do but kill a man once in a while."

"Guess you'd kill your own brother if Georges told you, wouldn't you?" said Johnny.

"I guess I would. Fact is, white man, that's why I'm down here. But it don' make no difference with me. Jest as soon kill 'em for Georges as the next man."

"Make you a bet, Bilbo."

Bilbo grunted. "What kind of a bet?"

"Bet you ten dollars you can't hit the riding light on that launch."

"You ain't got no ten dollars in the first place, white man."

"No? That's all you know about it. I buried it when I first came here."

"What light was that you was talkin' about jest now?"

"The starboard running light. You can't hit it, that's why you're hedging."

"Who's hedgin'?"

"You are," said Johnny.

Bilbo grunted and stood up. He moved out of the darkness like a greased panther, the rifle flung carelessly across the crook of his arm. "That ridin' light down there?"

"That's the one," said Johnny.

Bilbo grunted again, contemptuously. He threw the weapon to his shoulder.

Behind the black man, Heinie hurtled out of the underbrush. Bilbo turned. Johnny launched himself in a dive and struck up the rifle. It went off in the air, but the vicious man came down in a side sweep and hit Heinie under the ear. Heinie sprawled senseless on the sand.

Bilbo wheeled on Johnny, his great teeth gleaming against his ebon skull. The muzzle descended in a swift arc, spitting jagged flame.

Johnny ducked to one side and tried to snatch the muzzle. It eluded him. Powder singed his hair. He caught a greasy arm and threw it back. Bilbo chattered with rage and pain. The muzzle chopped down.

Johnny caught the other arm and jerked it. Bilbo screamed. The black was a tower of livid anger, all animal. Jerking the muzzle with both hands, Johnny secured the weapon and

41

staggered back, with Bilbo beating at him. Johnny went down into the sand. It was in his mouth, his hair. The hot, sweaty odor of the body on top of him was nauseating.

Feet pounded through the underbrush. Men were swearing, floundering through the inky night, still blinded by the lighted room they had just left.

Johnny felt the trigger guard and found the silver metal. He yanked it. The butt jarred his head. Bilbo sagged, coughing. The black tottered to his feet and then pitched headfirst into the water, to lie there inert. Johnny's throat burned from the clutch of savage fingers.

Trying to get up, Johnny saw the men coming at him. He threw the rifle to his shoulder and fired into the thickest of the mass. A pistol barked at him. Johnny's hand clawed out in search of Heinie. A sob caught deep in his chest and choked him.

"Heinie!" he moaned. "Heinie! Where—"

The mass loomed closer to him. Slugs bit through the night like hammering fists. The sand geysered under the impacts.

"Heinie!" Johnny shouted. "For God's—"

A voice was behind him. A voice, and the throb of an engine.

"Johnny. I've got him. I've got him, Johnny. Come on. Swim! Quick, Johnny!"

Alicia. Her tones were like a cool plunge. She had Heinie there in the boat. Alicia had Heinie. . . .

Johnny struggled for the water. At the edge he stumbled over Bilbo, a body without a head, the woolly hair lost in the waves. Johnny whirled and emptied the magazine at the men in the underbrush. They were yellow, they wouldn't tackle him. The rifle jarred his shoulder twice.

Taking it by the barrel, Johnny flung it toward the huts. He was lightheaded, walking on air. None of those slugs could touch him. Walking, refusing to run, he went out until the water was around his waist. Then, with a precise crawl, he struck out for the sputtering launch.

Phosphorus gleamed about him, burning in his wake. The bullets hammered the water, churning it. The lead traveled deep, leaving pencil lines of green fire behind them as they lanced through the depths.

Johnny swam evenly. He could hear shouts ashore. He could hear the motor sputtering, urging him on. He hadn't known the distance was so long. He struck on, gritting his teeth. The elation was gone now. This was merely hard, grueling work. This was the hard end of it. Like a log in the water, swimming, fighting off the imperious command of speed. Like a log drawing the fire of a dozen guns. They weren't shooting at Alicia, anyway.

He wondered how long he had been in the water. It might have been hours. Probably. He felt logy. No energy left. Had to find some. Had to get out there to Alicia and Heinie. Had to get back to the base and tell them where—tell them where—

Johnny knew he couldn't take another stroke. Better not hold them any longer. They'd get shot waiting for him. He could hear the motor throbbing. Better let them go. He'd gotten Bilbo, anyway. No use making Alicia—

A strong hand grabbed his shoulder. The fingers were like steel bands. Someone was pulling him up.

Johnny was hoisted over the gunwale and pitched into the bottom of the craft.

"Get going, Alicia!" shouted Heinie. "He's all right."

The launch jumped ahead like a struck thoroughbred. The water curved out behind them in a great V. The pistol flashes were lost to sight around the shoulder of land.

CHAPTER SIX

LAY TO!

THE world was draped with gossamer. Waves fled by, soon lost to sight astern. The fog was low and curling, obscuring even the V wake of the launch. Daylight had come some hours ago, but the sun fought a losing fight against the mist.

Eyes burning with strain, Johnny lay on the forward planking and stared ahead. Behind him, Heinie steered a cranky helm, his eyes on the jumping binnacle disk which swung through thirty degrees under the repeated impact of waves.

Alicia crawled forward to Johnny. Her amber red hair whipped damply in the speed-slashed air. Her powder blue uniform was beaded by spray, its Two-Continents insignia long tarnished. Her slim hand gripped Johnny's shoulder as a cross wave buffeted the craft.

"See anything, Johnny?"

"Not a thing. If this keeps up another hour, our position will be accurately plotted as lying somewhere off the Louisiana coast. Hungry?"

"No. I found those sea biscuits you laid out for me. I pretended the mold was jam."

"You poor kid."

Alicia laughed. "Don't 'poor kid' me. I have a hunch that

you didn't even eat that much. There's plenty of water, though, if you don't mind the taste of gasoline. I'm fast arriving at the conclusion that Georges and his men aren't human enough to eat or drink."

"Fix up that last word—they can drink, all right. What did Heinie say about our position?"

"I'm too much of a lady to repeat it."

Johnny grinned and crossed his hands under his chin. His eyes were fixed on the gray, endless wall through which they traveled. He was shivering a little from the damp cold of morning, but the crispness of the air, he considered, was recompense enough for that.

"One consolation," said Johnny, "if we don't know where we are, neither does Georges."

"Do you think he'll move Ferguson when he finds out that we've escaped?"

Johnny shrugged as well as any man can shrug while lying down. "Maybe and maybe not. We'll have to act quickly and trust to luck. Lord knows, if we don't nail the outfit where they are now, they'll be scattered through four points of the compass. There's a hanging waiting for each and every one of them since kidnaping went out of fashion."

"How about their dope smuggling?" asked Alicia.

"They won't even come up to trial for that, if I don't miss my guess. But if they happen to get away with the kidnaping, they'll still have twenty years apiece in Leavenworth. Georges has been at this dope smuggling since he was knee-high to a seagull. His father before him, too. Seems to run in the family."

"What happened to his father?"

46

Johnny laughed. "He was taken seriously ill and died. Scratched his hand on a nail and got lockjaw. There isn't any justice, Alicia."

"I'm beginning to think so. But listen, Johnny. If they move Ferguson, they'll take Mac and Billie and your crew with him and we might never—"

Johnny nodded, and then rapidly changed the subject. "I wish I could catch sight of a headland, anything. I'd know where we were, then."

"Why don't you just try to hit the coast?"

"That's what we're doing. Just that. But there are so many inlets and rivers along here that we'd run a chance of getting lost all over again. I'm trying to hit the mouth of the Mississippi if I can. Then we'll slam right into the base and get a patrol boat."

"But aren't there any patrol boats right out here?"

"Maybe. There's a regular patrol in this vicinity. We might even run into them, at this time of morning. The only trouble is that we may hit the CG-1004, and that would put us right into Coquelin's hands again."

Alicia tightened her mouth and fell silent. After a few minutes, she said, "I'll keep a lookout, if you want to take a rest. Your eyes look on fire."

"They are," agreed Johnny. "If you see anything, sing out good and loud."

Johnny went backward, crab fashion, until his worn shoes touched the cockpit rim. Then he rolled over and dropped down beside Heinie.

"How they going?" asked Johnny.

Heinie took his eyes off the compass for a moment. His glance was bleak. "I feel like a louse running around in a dark cellar. Ain't there ever any end to this fog?"

"I'll call up Jupiter Pluv, and have it removed immediately," said Johnny. "Want me to take the wheel?"

"I've got it."

"Okay. You didn't eat your sea biscuit."

Heinie smiled. "I'm saving it to throw at Georges if he turns up."

"We might run across Barney out here," said Johnny. "He has this run now."

"Barney Edwards? I don't like him. Takes his duty too much to heart. You'd think that guy ran the Coast Guard all by himself. It's 'Me and Admiral Baird' when Barney's around."

"He's not so bad," said Johnny. "Takes himself too seriously, but that's all right. He'll get places one of these days."

"He got places once. He was a warrant during the war, wasn't he?"

"Sure. They busted him down to seaman first class for messing up in a spy ring or something. He thought he was out to bust it up all by himself." Johnny sank down on the narrow seat and shielded his stinging eyes.

"You ever see that missing front tooth of his?"

Johnny shook his head without looking up.

"Well, after a private war we had, the tooth was missing in action. He always sort of held it against me."

"Boy!" said Johnny. "Never cross any of these old-time bosuns if you can help it. They're bad medicine. Even worse than ensigns. Barney Edwards and I crossed fists once about a year ago when I first came on this station. He had the CG-1000 and we were running out of the bay. He must have been asleep or something, because a launch cut across my bow and I had to swerve to keep from hitting it. Well, I slammed right into the 1000 before I knew what had happened. The damn fool didn't even make any attempt to get out of the way. Barney jumped me for it right then and there."

Johnny shook his head again. "Must have been some scrap! He's never been the same since."

Heinie laughed appreciatively, his eyes still on the jumping compass disk. For a moment he let his eyes wander over the small instrument panel before him.

"We're going to be out of gas in another fifteen minutes," he said.

"Have to run on sea water, I guess." Johnny got to his feet. "I'll go up and relieve Alicia." He scrambled over the cockpit rim and worked his way forward, clinging to the deck of the bucking launch.

"See anything?" asked Johnny.

"Nothing but fog," Alicia said. "Have we got plenty of gas and everything back there?"

"Plenty."

"That's good, because it looks like this fog will be with us some time. We might be halfway up the Mississippi to Chicago by this time, for all I know."

"Maybe so. The water's been yellow all morning, but then, it's that way a hundred miles out. Silt."

"Draw me pictures of it," smiled Alicia. "Do you suppose things will be all right ashore?"

49

"Why shouldn't they be?"

"I don't know. Intuition, I guess, but I've had an odd feeling that we're running into trouble. Something keeps telling me—"

"Forget it," said Johnny. "My record is good."

"I know, but just the same— Look, Johnny. What's that gray shape out there? See it?"

Johnny squinted through the thick blanket of vapor. At first he could see nothing, but when his eyes became accustomed to watching, he made out a thin shadow three points off the starboard bow.

"It's a ship," said Johnny.

"Fine. But isn't it small?"

"Yes. In fact, I'll bet you three to one it's a patrol boat."

"You mean—you mean, Georges might be—"

"Maybe. We won't lay to until we're damned sure of it, anyway." He raised himself on his elbows and called back to Heinie. "Slack off a couple knots. Ship off the starboard."

Heinie bobbed his head and kept his eyes on the binnacle.

Alicia held her hand above her eyes. "The stern is this way. Can you see any numbers?"

"It's a patrol boat, that's all I know. It might be the 1004, and again it might not. I'm taking no chances."

Above the droning thunder of the launch engine they could hear nothing, not even a loud megaphone call. The vessel became more distinct, but no markings were yet in evidence. Johnny held himself like a steel spring, his eyes nervous. He was conscious of Alicia's hand on his arm.

The patrol boat changed its course and curved away from

them, growing more indistinct. It circled, leaving a boiling wake in the choppy water, coming up astern of them.

"Maybe—" Johnny stopped, refusing to speculate on the ship's identity. The numbers were not visible.

Abruptly a geyser of water shot up ahead of the launch. Flame and smoke spat from the patrol boat's deck.

"Hell!" cried Johnny. "What's the big idea? Open her up, Heinie. That guy must be Georges!"

The engine's roar doubled. The stern crouched further down in the water. The spray of the bow arced up in two great screens. The waves beneath the stepped bottom were like mighty hammers thundering against the planking.

The patrol boat fired again. The shot fell twenty feet abeam of the speeding launch. They were drenched with cascading water.

"It's no use!" cried Johnny. "He's got the speed on us. Slack off, Heinie, slack off! He'll blow us out of the water, next shot!"

Heinie glanced over his shoulder and then jerked back on the throttle. He threw the launch into a long curve which swung it back alongside the patrol boat. They coasted to a stop, bobbing gently.

Johnny sighed with relief. The numbers CG-1000 were close beside them. This was not Georges Coquelin, but Barney Edwards.

A voice, bull-like, blasted at them. "Is that Trescott?"

"Right!" shouted Johnny.

"Come over alongside us. Don't try anything funny or I'll sink you with one shot. Get me?"

Heinie sent an alarmed glance toward his chief and then glowered up at the red face which seemed to float, detached, above them. Heinie threw in the clutch and edged over to the gray hull.

"Well?" demanded Johnny. "What's eating you now?"

Barney Edwards nodded with satisfaction. "Trying a stall, huh? Trying to—oh, hell, Trescott, don't try anything like that with me! You're not smart enough, see? I see you even picked up a dame."

Johnny reached up and gripped the line along the rail. He threw himself over the side and stamped down to the deck of the CG-1000. He stopped in front of Edwards.

"Lay off the wisecracks," said Johnny. "Take us back to the base immediately."

"Take him back to the base!" Edwards guffawed. "Hey, Jake. Drop down there and see if anything's in that launch before we sink it."

"We know you're funny, Edwards, and I'm laughing." Johnny scowled. "What's the idea? Still got a grudge against me? That it?"

Edwards jabbed his hand to his side and yanked out a .45. "You're smart, Trescott—damned smart—but you can't get around me. You didn't stop when I called to you, did you?"

"I didn't hear you," snapped Johnny.

"Swell excuse, a swell excuse! You didn't even stop when I fired a shot over your bows. You know what that means. You were trying to get away, weren't you? Trying to give me the slip."

Alicia and Heinie climbed up over the side and stood beside

GET
4 FREE BOOKS!

You can have the titles in the Stories from the Golden Age delivered to your door by signing up for the book club. Start today, and we'll send you **4 FREE BOOKS** (worth $39.80) as your reward.

◄◦►

The collection includes 80 volumes (book or audio) by master storyteller L. Ron Hubbard in the genres of science fiction, fantasy, mystery, adventure and western, originally penned for the pulp magazines of the 1930s and '40s.

◄◦►

YES! ☐

Sign me up for the Stories from the Golden Age Book Club and send me my first book for $9.95 with my **4 FREE BOOKS** (FREE shipping). I will pay only $9.95 each month for the subsequent titles in the series. Shipping is FREE and I can cancel any time I want to.

First Name _____ Middle Name _____ Last Name _____

Address _____

City _____ State _____ ZIP _____

Telephone _____ E-mail _____

Credit/Debit Card #: _____

Card ID# (last 3 or 4 digits): _____ Exp Date: _____ / _____

Date (month/day/year) _____ / _____ / _____

Signature: _____

Comments: _____

Check here ✔ to receive a FREE Stories from the Golden Age catalog or go to: **GoldenAgeStories.com**.

Thank you!

© 2011 Galaxy Press, LLC. All Rights Reserved. Pulp magazine cover artwork are reprinted with permission from Argosy Communications, Inc.; Penny Publications, LLC; Hachette Filipacchi Media; and Condé Nast Publications.

BUSINESS REPLY MAIL
FIRST-CLASS MAIL   PERMIT NO. 75738   LOS ANGELES CA

POSTAGE WILL BE PAID BY ADDRESSEE

GOLDEN AGE BOOK CLUB
GALAXY PRESS
7051 HOLLYWOOD BLVD
LOS ANGELES CA 90028-9771

NO POSTAGE
NECESSARY
IF MAILED
IN THE
UNITED STATES

Please fold here and send in.

JOIN THE
STORIES
FROM THE
GOLDEN AGE
BOOK CLUB!

#1 New York Times Bestselling Author
L. RON HUBBARD

Galaxy Press
7051 Hollywood Blvd., Suite 200 • Hollywood, CA 90028
1-877-8GALAXY (1-877-842-5299)
To sign up online, go to:
GoldenAgeStories.com

Stories
from the
Golden Age
by
L. Ron Hubbard

FREE BOOKS offer available for a limited time only. Prices set in US dollars only. Non-US residents, please call 1-323-466-7815 for pricing information or go to GoldenAgeStories.com. Sales tax where applicable. Terms, prices and conditions subject to change. Subscription subject to acceptance. You may cancel your subscription at any time. Galaxy Press reserves the right to reject any order or cancel any subscription. If under 18, a parent or guardian must sign.

the deckhouse, waiting. Heinie was plainly worried, Alicia puzzled.

The man called Jake threw three packages up to the deck and then followed them. He juggled a fourth in his hand.

"We don't have to open it to know what this is," said Jake.

Nevertheless, Edwards ripped it along the side and then laughed. "Dope. Heroin in phials. I suppose somebody gave this to you to hold while he got on a streetcar!"

"You fool!" snapped Johnny. "I stole this launch, and I can't help its cargo."

"That's a new one. That's a new one, all right. So you stole the boat. You admit that, too."

"If you're putting on a show for my benefit, Edwards—"

"I'm not putting on any show." Edwards turned to three of his men. "Keep 'em covered, you guys. And you, Jake, see if you can't find me some wrist irons. Oh, we've got these beauties dead to rights. They don't stop when we fire a shot, and they say they stole the boat. You heard them admit that."

Johnny was suddenly struck with the idea. "You mean you think I—you think I stole the CG-1004. Why, you're crazy, Edwards—crazy as hell! Just because we had a little scrap—"

"It's no good to plead about old times, Trescott," Edwards assured him. "I've got you dead to rights and you know it. Got you in the act of smuggling dope into the coast on your own. You tried to evade arrest, didn't you?"

"You've got orders to this effect?" demanded Johnny.

"Orders!" bellowed Edwards. "Plenty of 'em. General orders

to all ships and stations to arrest one John Trescott and crew whenever and wherever sighted."

"But for *what*?" cried Heinie, unable to stand it any longer.

"For piracy on the high seas. For murder. And for the kidnaping of J. G. Ferguson for ransom. For using the uniform of the Coast Guard and a Coast Guard ship for the purposes of piracy. For—"

"Good God! You don't believe that, do you?" shouted Johnny.

"No time to talk now. We're getting underway for the base right quick. This is one day's work they won't forget. They'll rate me plenty. Hey, you guys! Take this bunch below and lock 'em tight! Don't even let 'em talk. Get me?"

CHAPTER SEVEN

PRISONERS

HAROLD CLARKE'S briefcase was shiny in the blue cell light. As shiny as his glasses and his carefully polished shoes. Tall and gaunt, he was more a filing case than a man.

"The authorities have matters well in hand," said Harold Clarke in his dry, precise voice. "I am convinced that you have no authentic message for me, but since you have requested my presence, I am here."

Johnny Trescott glanced sideways at Heinie and then back at Ferguson's secretary. "You won't even run a small chance to get your boss back?"

"There is probably some trickery involved. I cannot interfere with the officials, the charges are far too serious."

"But I'm not asking you for money, Clarke. I haven't said a word about money. All I'm asking for is a lawyer, and a good one. How about it?"

"I have no authority to expend funds in your behalf. I am indebted to you for nothing." Clarke hoisted his briefcase under his bony arm and looked anxiously down the gray corridor, making sure of the guard.

"Well, what are you waiting for?" said Johnny.

Clarke turned. "I beg your pardon?"

"Get out," said Johnny, softly. "If you don't, I might change my mind and strangle you."

Beneath the lenses, Clarke's eyes seemed to pop. He rattled the bars of the door, afraid to take his eyes from Johnny. A Coast Guardsman clumped up and unlocked the cell. Clarke hurried out.

A moment later a car roared outside the brig. The gears crashed, and then the motor dwindled into nothing. Heinie grinned.

"Brave guy, that Clarke!"

Johnny cupped his chin in his palms and stared out into the gray passage. "He was, in his own right. If you were Clarke, you'd have done the same thing. After all, Heinie, the papers have been pretty bitter about this thing."

"I wish they'd hang us or something—anything! I'm getting bored. This makes three days just sitting in here looking at the walls."

"Wonder what happened to Alicia."

Heinie spread his hands. "I don't know. The last I saw of her, she was headed for town in the commanding officer's car. Don't suppose she—"

"Turned evidence on us? Good Lord, no!" Johnny was aghast. "She saw that she couldn't get us anywhere by going to jail with us, so she kept her mouth shut. She's up to something. You can bet your back pay on it."

"I haven't got any back pay. The old boys took us off the records. There's no justice in this old woman's world, Johnny."

Footsteps scuffed toward them and a red face jumped into being between the bars. It was Barney Edwards.

"Just came up to tell you," said Edwards, "that your summary comes up in the morning. A summary court-martial. That's what you're going to get. Hanging."

"Well," said Heinie, "thanks for the news. Damned thoughtful of you to come around with such cheerful tidings. Have they made you an admiral yet?"

"No. They boosted me, though, and they'll boost me again. Just dropped in to tell you."

Johnny shifted his weight, and the rusty bunk creaked. "I suppose it's no more patrol for you, then. Living off the fat of the land, huh?"

"Who, me?" cried Edwards. "Not me, I'm not. I'm going out on patrol tonight. In fact right away. I'm going to locate that boat you jailbirds swiped. And then there'll be hell to pay, take it from me."

Johnny leaned forward, eagerly, about to tell Edwards where he could find the CG-1004. But in a moment he relaxed.

"That's fine. Wish you a lot of luck," he said.

"Luck! There's no luck to it!" Edwards snorted. "Takes brains and hard work to get along in the Coast Guard."

Heinie laughed out loud. Johnny grinned.

"Well, I guess that puts you aces up," said Johnny.

"It sure does, and then some. I'm going to show them how it's supposed to be done. In an hour I'll be putting out to sea in the 1000, all loaded down."

"Fuel tanks full?" asked Johnny.

"All the way up."

Johnny nodded. "Well, don't let us keep you waiting, Barney. Be sure and keep your brass shiny—you've got enough of it."

Barney Edwards was gone, and through the small barred window, Heinie was watching the dock and the CG-1000.

"Boy!" said Heinie. "I'd certainly love to get out to sea in that tub. We'd make Georges walk fast and far."

"I almost told him where the 1004 was located," said Johnny, "but I'll be doggoned if I'll let that glory-snatcher grab off the credit for it. He'd fix it so we wouldn't have had a thing to do with it."

"Here comes Lieutenant Maitland," whispered Heinie.

Lieutenant Maitland, counsel for the defense, entered with stiff uncompromising stride. He had been appointed to his task much against his will, and the fact was clearly etched in his sunburned face. He sparkled with gold braid and distaste.

When he entered the cell, he eyed his two "clients" with disgust. Garbed as they were in prison dungarees, they were two uninteresting units which comprised a distasteful case.

Johnny and Heinie stood up, in deference to his rank, but Maitland either forgot or refused to give the order "At ease."

"Tomorrow," said Maitland, "you will be up for a summary court-martial. Admiral Baird is coming down from Washington to make certain that matters are speedily carried out."

Johnny's lips were stiff. "Didn't the lieutenant make any effort to hold it off until we get some evidence or until the so-called Phantom is captured?"

"Are you criticizing my ability as counsel?" rapped the officer.

"Yes," said Johnny, unmoving. "You should do everything in your power to prevent a hasty trial."

Maitland licked his lips and glared. "Your record is none too savory now, Trescott, without adding insubordination to the list."

"To hell with insubordination," flared Johnny. "You haven't made any effort to cooperate with us in getting everything straightened out. I offered to tell you where you could find the CG-1004, but you turned me down."

"You can make no bargains with justice, Trescott. Remember that at your trial. I will have to ask you to be silent tomorrow."

"Oh, you will!" said Johnny. "Tomorrow I'm going to get hold of newspapermen and spread this farce all over the country!"

"Interesting," replied Maitland, his nostrils quivering. "Very interesting. But it so happens that you won't be near any newspapermen. They are not to be admitted—they never are where court-martials are concerned. Tomorrow I expect the verdict of hanging to be handed down."

"You mean you hope to see it," said Johnny.

"You are obnoxious, Trescott," Maitland rapped. "You impede my efforts to defend you. You thought it was a good idea to take the 1004 and commit piracy on the high seas. Tomorrow you are going to find out that it wasn't so good after all. If you want to know the truth, I'm glad, damned glad, that they'll make you dance higher than a kite."

"What a swell lawyer!" sighed Heinie.

Maitland whirled on him. "You two are utterly lawless. You have no respect for higher authority. You—"

"Your record is none too savory now, Trescott,
without adding insubordination to the list."

Johnny interrupted. "Higher authority, did you say? Listen, Lieutenant. On that score I've only got this to say. Thank God for the enlisted men of the Coast Guard!"

"Meaning?" grated Maitland.

"You don't have to look far to get my meaning, Lieutenant. If you'd attend a few less pink teas you'd know something about what we're up against. You'd know what we've had to face on the high seas."

"I'll have you—" began Maitland.

"You're letting them hang us now. A few minor offenses don't make any difference to us."

Maitland executed a perfect about-face. Behind him the cell door slammed, its bars shivering. The stamping feet echoed in the passage.

"Anybody but him!" said Heinie. "It's just our luck. Out of all the swell guys in this outfit, we have to get picked up by Edwards, and they appoint Maitland to act as our counsel. Ain't that hell, Johnny?"

"Pretty rotten. But there wasn't any luck about it. The job of counsel is a tough one, and everybody thinks we're as guilty as sin, and nobody else likes Maitland, so they handed the job over to him. And as for Barney picking us up, we knew that before it happened. But I do wish it had been almost anybody else."

Heinie sighed and slumped down on his bunk. "And all because Georges Coquelin has white hair and blue eyes! My God, Johnny, that description would fit any one of a hundred thousand men!"

"Sure it would. But you've got to think of this. A Coast

Guard boat runs crazy, boarding and looting. We disappear at the same time. After that the public gets leery of the Coast Guard and refuses to place any confidence in it. That was a tough blow, after all the underhand propaganda that was shot around during prohibition days. We no more than pull out of that—I mean the Coast Guard—than the public gets hot about this Phantom."

"Funny Georges hasn't done anything since we were taken in. Do you suppose that he knows they'll nail us?"

"It's in all the papers," said Johnny, "and it's been released through all of the radio dispatches. He's picked it up all right. And he'll do one of two things."

"And what are those?"

Johnny slapped his palm, his eyes narrow. "By golly, I just happened to get this figured out! It's bad!"

"What is?"

Johnny shook his head. "Bad. Georges will be able to approach vessels, now that the scare is over. He'll repaint the numbers on the bow. He'll blast out their radio masts and then board the boats and loot them. After that, he'll have to sink them with all hands."

"Good Lord! You think he'd do that?"

"Sure he would, no question about it. Remember Henri? That puts us right up against it, Heinie, right smack against it. Ferguson is out there. He'll have to be rescued."

"That—"

"I know, I know. But he'll have to be rescued anyway. They'll ask for ransom after we've been hung. Either that, or, more likely, they'll kill Ferguson and drop the matter, rather than take the blame on themselves for it. They'll kill him, that's what they'll do."

"And Billie and Mac and our boys!" groaned Heinie.

"It amounts to this. We'll have to get out of here somehow. It will mean trouble in plenty, but we'll have to make it. We can't let those poor devils die, and we'll have to act before Georges takes in any more ships."

"To say nothing of saving our own necks, Johnny. Don't forget those. It's no fun to hang."

Johnny stood up and stared out into the night beyond the small barred window. The cool breath of the sea was fanning his tanned cheek.

CHAPTER EIGHT

INTO THE FOG

At ten o'clock, fog began to seep in from the water. Great swirling blankets dropped down over the station. The lights were hazy dots ringed with golden bands. A ship's bell softly tolled the hour, four strokes, two double beats.

Johnny roved the cell, pausing occasionally to peer out of the window. As the echo of the bell died away, he turned to the sprawled Heinie.

"Funny," Johnny said. "Edwards hasn't put to sea yet. He said he was leaving in an hour, too."

"Maybe his sense of duty failed him."

"Not his! I wonder what's the matter."

"You better start worrying about Alicia, Johnny. She hasn't even been in here to see us since we landed."

"Probably up to something—I'd like to know what. I think she's playing a wise hand. If she came in here, Heinie, they'd know she was hand in glove with us. But if she hands out a sob line to them, they'll think she's the best ever—which she is."

"You think a lot of her, don't you?"

Johnny nodded. "You know it, sailor."

Heinie rose in a sitting position, about to remark upon it further. But he clapped his hands over his head and said, "Ouch!"

Something jingled against the stone floor. Johnny dropped to his knees, feeling for it. His eyes were eager and he held his breath. An instant later he stood up, holding a dozen keys by their ring.

"What the hell—?" began Heinie.

"Shut up, you ape. These are the keys to the cell!"

"But why should—"

"Alicia," whispered Johnny. "She must have stolen them right out of the guardroom." He stepped to the door, ran his arm through the bars, and in an instant metal grated.

The cell door swung creakingly back. The two were in the corridor, stepping softly.

They reached the guardroom, but it was empty.

"There should be a CPO here," breathed Heinie.

"There he is." Johnny pointed at a pair of feet which protruded out from under a table. The chief petty officer was breathing heavily, a swelling bump on the back of his head.

"Alicia couldn't have knocked him!" said Heinie, goggling.

Johnny picked up the fallen guard's .45 and strapped it to his own waist. He echoed the motto of the Coast Guard, *"Semper Paratus."* Always Prepared.

That done, Johnny stepped to the outer door and looked long into the fog, puzzled. Heinie stepped outside and beckoned.

"Come on, dumbhead!" said Heinie. "Somebody'll come along any minute!"

Johnny strode forward, taking advantage of the shadows against the building side, groping through the heavy mist. A shape loomed before him and he dodged, gun ready.

66

"Put it away," said the shape in a hoarse voice. "Alicia's waiting for us down at the dock."

Johnny beckoned to Heinie. They began to run, their feet padding over the gravel. The bulk of the patrol boat leaped up at them.

A hand snatched at Johnny's arm. He whirled, and in the space of an instant he had found Alicia and had kissed her.

"Johnny, Johnny. It was forever!" she whispered, vibrantly.

"And ever." He released her. "Is the ship—?"

"Get aboard. It's cleared." She pushed him forward. He felt for the gangway and clattered up to the deck.

In the pilothouse, Barney Edwards lay in the corner, trussed, gagged and glowering. Johnny grinned and scooped him up. He raced back to the dock and threw Edwards to the planking.

"There's glory for you," hissed Johnny, and went back aboard the ship.

The engines were turning over. A mysterious man was casting off the lines. Heinie had taken over the helm and stood tense and waiting, expecting immediate pursuit.

The dock slid away, a gray ghost. The lights became dim and were replaced by a gentle glow against the sky—New Orleans. The two Sterling 200-hp engines throbbed valiantly under the planks. A buoy slipped past, clanging dolefully. A headland rose up and fell away. The tug of a current caught at their bows as they met the first waves of the Gulf.

It was not until then that Johnny left the bridge. He found Alicia standing beside the one-pounder, looking ahead. He could see by the deckhouse lights that she was crying.

"Why—why, what's the matter?" said Johnny.

"Just—just happy, that's all. Just so happy I can't stand it!"

He patted her shoulder, feeling the inadequacy of the gesture. "Forget it, Alicia. We're out to sea and heading for Georges Coquelin's base. Everything is going to be fine in no time at all."

"I know it—that's why I'm crying."

"Listen," said Johnny. "Why and how did you do all this?"

"The why is easy—you know why I did it. The how—well, the how was easy, too." She dabbed at her eyes with a thin white square of linen and then straightened up. The blue serge sport suit made her melt back into the darkness. Only her face was visible. Her blue eyes and her finely chiseled features. She was smiling now.

"That man that met you," said Alicia, "that was Joe Burgan. He's a rigger for Two-Continents."

"For Two-Continents!"

"Yes. You see, I had to have a crew for this boat. I knew none of the regular sailors would put out with you after all that's happened, and these men—well, I guess they have faith in me. I've done them a lot of favors from time to time. The fellow that's running the engines is Dave Whitman. He's chief mechanic for Two-Continents at Miami. He knows all about Diesels.

"Then," she continued, "I located two fishermen, and I thought that would be enough crew, with you and Heinie."

"Sure, it's six men. That's all we ever carry on these boats. But how did you pay them? They wouldn't leave their jobs just like that."

"Oh, you'd be surprised at a woman's wiles, Johnny—terribly

surprised. But I did promise them money. Five thousand dollars apiece."

"Five thousand—good Lord, Alicia, where—"

"Oh, I had to gamble that. If Ferguson's still alive, he'll have to pay it. If he isn't—well, that's just a chance we'll have to take, I guess."

Johnny laughed, and Alicia joined in.

"Of course," said Johnny, "it's no laughing matter. But it feels good to be free again. Feels good to feel the salt air, even though it's foggy. And best of all, you're here. We'll make a stab at getting Georges."

"We have a fair chance, too," Alicia replied. "If we can get there when the patrol boat isn't in the cove, we'll be able to do things."

Johnny nodded. "Have you any other dope you're holding out?"

"No, not that I know of."

"I mean about shipping. What steamer is due in here tonight?"

"Oh, yes," she said. "I did check up on that. It's foggy and Georges might be out, that it? The *City of New Orleans* is due at the anchorage at eleven."

"She always carries a pretty fair number of rich people," said Johnny. "She isn't very big, but then, I don't think Georges will try for anything over pint-size. You see, I figure Georges will make a stab at small boats. He'll blast out their radio masts first, and then after he loots them, he'll put a bomb in their hold and blow them up. That way there won't be a hint of the fact that the so-called Phantom is still at work."

69

Johnny stepped to the door of the deckhouse. "Listen, Heinie, keep a good check on your course and steer for the outer steamer anchorage."

"Think we'll pick up Georges out there?"

"You never can tell. We'll head for it, full speed."

"Okay, Johnny."

The patrol boat surged through the waves, heading straight into the swells. The deck bobbed gently up and down in a slow waltz.

Johnny's blond head was bowed over a chart. The compasses glittered in his hand like twin foils. Island by island, he was limiting the possible stronghold of Georges Coquelin. Finally he picked up a blue pencil and made two gashes on the yellow hydrographic map.

Johnny stood up and threw the pencil down on the table. "Heinie, if we don't pick him up out here at the anchorage, we'll still have a pretty fair chance of hitting his base."

Heinie glanced at Johnny out of his eye corners. "Yeah. But I'm worried about just one thing, Johnny. If Georges had any brains, he'd kill Ferguson and Mac and Billie and our boys. If they're still alive, their testimony will be the thing."

Johnny nodded slowly, his sea blue eyes deep and thoughtful. "I see what you mean. You think that grabbing off Georges himself isn't going to do us a bit of good."

"Right. It won't mean a thing. Georges will put up all kinds of squawks to get off. It will be his word against ours, and I'm telling you, our word won't be worth a plugged *centavo* after this little business of boat stealing tonight."

"Then you don't think we're in such a swell spot, after all." Johnny went to the door and looked out. The air was no longer cool. "We'll have to get every one of them in order to get off, I guess. We won't be able to sail around forever and a day in this tub. If we don't get Ferguson back alive, it's all up with the lot of us. He's the boy that will turn the tide in our favor."

"We can try, anyway," said Heinie. "They'd hang us otherwise. Maybe they will, yet." He glanced up at the barometer and its chart. "Glass is falling a little. We'll be in for a squall before morning."

Johnny sniffed at the fog. It had a flat, dead taste. The Gulf seemed calm, too calm. The swells that swept by on either side were greasy.

Johnny found Alicia in the bows, seated on a bitt.

"We're in for a blow," he told her. "But it's all right with me."

"Let 'er blow!" Alicia smiled. "They'll play the devil finding us in rough weather."

"Maybe. They've got a hundred-and-sixty-five-footer back at the base. That thing would make short work out of us if it ever caught sight of this scow."

"There's a whole navy ahead," said Alicia, "so don't worry about any more fights than that, if you can help it."

"You mean the cruiser," said Johnny. "Sure. I know it's going to be tough, but we'll have speed this time, and when I've got one of these ships going full ahead, I can make a monkey out of anything bigger. They won't even get the canvas off that three-inch gun."

71

"I wish we both believed that."

Johnny laughed, somewhat nervously. His palms were moist and hot, and his muscles felt jerky. He always felt that way just before he went into action. The mugginess of the night wasn't improving his tension.

Ahead he could see a blur of lights through the gray curtain. "That's the ship *City of New Orleans*, I guess. I wonder if they've had any—"

The jarring thunder of pistol shots slapped across the water. Somewhere aboard the anchored *City of New Orleans* a woman screamed.

PURSUIT

JOHNNY'S hands clawed at the breech of the one-pounder. Someone was beside him, cramming a shell into the weapon—Alicia! Johnny yanked the muzzle into position. Powder flame blasted the swirls of fog. The empty brass cylinder clattered to the deck, smoke wreathing from its black mouth.

Ahead the CG-1004 was a dull line against the dark steamer side. At this range of a hundred yards it was impossible to miss. Men were scrambling down the Jacob's ladder, back to the renegade's deck.

The one-pounder roared again. The clang of shells into the breech was an anvil chorus, punctuated by the battering explosion of powder. The weapon was hot under Johnny's fists.

Heinie was swerving the CG-1000 into better range. From the 1004 the crackle of rifle fire dotted the blackness. The sound was dead in the leaden air.

Splinters geysered out of the renegade's deck. In the light of the deckhouse, Georges Coquelin jerked at the helm, his slitted eyes transfixed by the vision of a bow sliding at him so swiftly that a crash seemed unavoidable.

The 1004 leaped away. The Jacob's ladder caught in the rail and slithered down to splash into the sea. Coquelin's other

73

one-pounder was smashing out its defiance. The projectiles glanced off the sea and whined away, turning over and over.

Johnny aimed at the fleeing craft, aimed at the lighted ports forward. But it was as if they had sensed his intent. The yellow patches blinked out.

A great swirl of mist passed between the boats, like a numbing blanket. For a moment the Phantom's stern was visible. Then the renegade was gone.

Out of the south came a moan of wind, forerunner of the coming storm, deadening all other sound. The fog, close-packed, swooped upward and down again, erasing even the *City of New Orleans'* lights.

Johnny, his hand on the lanyard, waited, striving to pierce the thickness of the curtain, striving to catch the faintest glimmer of sound. But it was an impossible feat. The Phantom could have changed its course a dozen times. It was lost.

Johnny wiped a black-grimed hand across his face and left a dark streak just below his hair. "No use to try to get them now."

"No use," echoed Heinie, from the open window of the deckhouse. "We'd better head for their base."

"Swing back alongside the steamer," Johnny ordered. "We'll see if they're all right."

The CG-1000 came around in a welter of foam. It charged back toward the black shadow against the sullen sky. With reversed engines, it bobbed to a stop under the steamer's bridge.

"Are you all right up there?" shouted Johnny.

A distraught face peered down at them. "We're all right. They shot the mate and wrecked our radio."

"No bombs planted?"

The face shook in a negative. "No. But they were ready with them. Thanks a lot, buddy."

"Okay," Johnny replied. Over his shoulder he said, "Get going, Heinie. I marked the course on the chart. We'll have to beat that devil to his base."

The CG-1000 darted ahead, ducked under the looming stern of the steamer, and shot out for the south, straight into the teeth of the rising gale. . . .

Before the onslaught of the storm, the legions of fog were swept back, routed. The visibility increased. The sea, lashed into bucking froth by the wind, became ebon. The sky was dark, the low clouds scudded onward into the north to overwhelm the coast.

One of the fishermen, a Cajun called Jaques, stood at the wheel. His inky eyes wandered from the binnacle to the foredeck. He was used to steering by the sails. His gaze occasionally took in the slim straight body of Johnny Trescott, who stood facing the wind. There were both appraisal and doubt in the Cajun's face. He did not fully understand just why he was here. He did not realize that the letters across the back of Johnny's blue jumper branded the man as an escaped prisoner. The Cajun called Jaques could not read. But he could steer a ship through a howling storm, and he knew both the meaning and the joy of a fight.

"You know Barque Island, don't you?" said Johnny.

The Cajun batted his eyes, then nodded. "Look like a ship. Sure, I know him."

"That's where we're heading."

"Bad place. Sometime fish ship get beached there. Crew all die. Funny thing. What you want with Barque Island?"

"Georges Coquelin is there. Know him?"

Jaques stared, forgetting in that instant that the wheel was a live, spinning thing. "Sure. Sure. Georges Coquelin. Plenty bad, that feller."

"Watch the helm," reproved Johnny. "We'll ship a sea if you don't keep headed into it."

Jaques stabbed his inky eyes down into the binnacle and kept them there. Small lights of excitement flickered across his face.

Johnny moved toward the hatch and swung himself through the opening into the glare of the engine room. Dave Whitman, chunky, bland and intent, stood by the port Diesel, monkey wrench in hand.

"Getting everything you can out of those?" asked Johnny.

"You bet. You're damned right I am. Miss Alicia was just down and told me where we were heading."

Johnny smiled. "I'd like to have you for an engineer, steady."

Dave Whitman glowed under the compliment. To hide a slight embarrassment, he stooped down and started to check the oiling system. Johnny left him there and went aft.

Alicia and Heinie were drinking coffee and eating roast beef sandwiches. Alicia poured out a cup for Johnny.

"Heavy weather," Alicia commented.

"Sure. But I've seen worse. That gives us the advantage over Georges. These boats are cranky." Johnny took a long drag at the scalding black fluid. "If you don't know every rivet in them you have a tough time bucking a headwind. We'll make it there in about three-quarters of the time it will take Georges."

"Sure we will," said Heinie, his mouth filled with roast beef. "But what are we going to do about it after we get there?"

"I think we'll land and see if we can't take Ferguson and the others off before Georges gets there. Then we'll stand to and wait for Georges to roll in."

"And blast him," said Heinie, swallowing and smiling at the same time. "I've got a machine gun all oiled up for you."

"That's swell." Johnny looked toward the far end of the cabin, where the gun was braced against the wall. "We'll have an advantage over the boys ashore, a big advantage. They'll think we're Georges until we tell them different."

Alicia sighed. "This suspense is killing me. If we don't find Ferguson alive, we'll never stand a chance of proving you two innocent. Getting the others and wiping out the base won't mean a thing."

Over their heads the electric light glowed softly. Alicia's amber red hair threw back small fires. The machine gun thumped with the pitch of the boat, as rhythmic as the throb of the engines. The wind through the radio mast was a screaming, moaning thing which swept through a dozen octaves in half as many seconds.

Joe Burgan appeared in the door. "This guy Jaques says we're getting right close to Barque Island."

CHAPTER TEN

JOHNNY COMES BACK

IT had been but a few days before—their escape. But now, sliding around the headland into the cove, all that seemed a thousand years away. Johnny felt only a tingle of anticipation. He remembered only the pistol shots which had streaked through the water beside him that other night. They had tried to kill him then. Anything he did to them in return would be amply justified now.

The beach was a faintly visible stretch of gray through the spattering rain. One single light glowed behind the shielding trees. They were waiting for Georges to return.

Before the CG-1000 had fully entered the landlocked area of water, a lantern came from the undergrowth and swung back and forward. A man was walking there. The Diesels had been heard.

Johnny sent the other Cajun forward to release the anchors. The chains roared out of the hawse pipes. The momentum of the patrol boat carried it around in a half circle until the stern pointed to the shore. They ran out the davits and swung the wherry into the water.

The surface of the cove was calm. The rain rippled before the blast of the wind. The wherry bobbed at the 1000 gunwale.

Johnny dropped into the bow with the machine gun. The cartridge belt dripped water and the breech glistened. Heinie pulled out the oars and stroked swiftly toward the beach. The lantern was there, waiting for them.

Johnny's throat was tight and dry. He was afraid that Georges had killed Ferguson. If the others were dead, all this foray was in vain.

The lantern bobbed impatiently. A swirl of water lapped high up the wherry's bow. Heinie was pulling with all his strength and skill.

Johnny leaped out on the sand. By the lantern light he saw it was Little Joe—little only where his head was concerned. His body was a great ill-shapen mass splashed by the rays. His shirt was open at the collar, displaying matted hair.

"What you back so soon for?" he demanded.

Johnny stepped closer. Little Joe raised the lantern and peered at Johnny's face.

"My God! Trescott!" It was the last speech ever made by Little Joe. He stabbed his hand toward a low-swung holster. The pistol came out, halfway.

Striding ahead, the machine gun thrown over the crook of his arm, Johnny fired a short burst. Little Joe's pistol sent a slug deep into the sand.

Over his shoulder Johnny said, "Get back to the ship, Heinie. They heard that. Stand off to wait for Georges."

"But you'll be—" Heinie stopped. Johnny had already disappeared into the fringe of trees. The body of Little Joe sprawled against the sand beside the guttering lantern. The rain pounded against the back of the sodden shirt.

Johnny knew the paths. He had had three months to learn them, and through all those three months he had somehow known that he would have need for that knowledge. He was back. The fact was like wine. He was back with a machine gun in his hands, and with the rain and night to protect him.

He heard the patrol boat hoist its anchors. The Diesels throbbed above the beat of the rain through the jungle. The CG-1000 was swinging out to sea to wait for Georges.

Johnny strode down toward a shadow against the night. It was the hut where Ferguson should be. But no lights were there. No sound. Nothing but the slither of rain through leaves and fronds.

Johnny kicked in the door. "Ferguson!" he hissed.

Only the drip of water running through the eaves. Johnny lit a match, carefully hiding its glare, and stared at the bunk. The match burned his fingers and he dropped it, almost without noticing the pain. He was suddenly nerveless.

The bunk was empty. Ferguson was gone. To Johnny that meant but one thing. It meant that they had killed the financier rather than bear the brunt of the investigation a ransom request would have brought. And they had killed Billie and Mac and all the rest. . . .

The dread hopelessness of the situation settled down over Johnny like a sullen cloud. All this, then, had been in vain. He had come back, he had stolen a ship, he had branded himself. There would be no hope of reprieve or acquittal now. They would track him down. That he had wiped out Georges Coquelin would mean nothing. Even if he took Coquelin alive, it still meant nothing.

Johnny ran a wet hand across his face. He felt as though he were struggling through the depths of a hideous nightmare.

A flashlight lashed through the door at him. He whirled, his fingers reaching the machine-gun trips. The weapon stuttered. The flashlight dropped.

A wailing voice came through the rain. A voice which went away. "It's Trescott! Trescott!"

Johnny hefted the machine gun and stepped out through the door. He avoided the man who sprawled there, but he retrieved the flashlight. The slugs hadn't touched it.

Johnny knew that only one course was left open to him. He could wipe out Georges Coquelin's base, and he *would* wipe it out. If he died trying— He grinned bitterly to himself. He wouldn't indulge in any heroics. Johnny stepped out along the path that led to the main huts.

The wind was high. It did not seem to reach down into the mass of vegetation. It stayed aloof, howling through the treetops like a banshee. The rain, driven in slanting sheets, blotted out the lights ahead for seconds at a time. The path was gutted by the running streams.

Johnny's dungarees were black with water. His shoes held in more rain than they kept out. Vines clawed at him, as if to stay his progress. A jagged bolt of lightning lit the world for an infinitesimal space of time. The rumbling thunder growled along the vague horizon.

As if in echo to the roar, the spiteful bark of a one-pounder jarred through the rain. It was a signal. Its repeated reports were drowned in a clattering spurt of rifle and machine-gun fire.

Johnny stopped and knelt, trying to pierce the jungle

with his eyes. He did not know for certain, but he could guess that Heinie was tangling with Georges Coquelin. Johnny knew the advantage of a surprise attack, and he knew Heinie's deftness with a one-pounder. He had no doubts that Heinie would win out.

Before the last swirl of thought had passed through Johnny's mind, the sea was again silent. Johnny smiled, and got to his feet. Confidently he strode ahead to finish the attack on land.

Perhaps it was the tone of the wind, perhaps the persistent quiet that lay over the water, but Johnny began to frown. Perhaps all was not well out there.

He fought his way to the water's edge and stared at the overcast sea. He could see nothing, hear nothing. An electric shock hit him between the shoulder blades. The force was so physical that, for an instant, he imagined that he had been shot. Then he realized that it had merely been a dread premonition.

If Georges had won out there, then Alicia would be in his hands. The patrol boat would be sunk. And Johnny would be right back where he had started from three months ago.

He hitched at the machine gun, a determined light playing in his eyes. He had caught the vaguest suggestion of a sound. Sand grating on wood.

Crouching, he listened for a repetition of the noise. The rain hammered at him, cloaked him in blackness. He inched his way down the beach, waiting, ready for anything. A splash came to him, faintly, as though someone was swimming in the cove. But perhaps that had been only a trick of his imagination.

After an interval of five leaden minutes, Johnny was frowning, plainly worried. No rocket signal had soared up to tell him that everything was all right. No lights were out there to tell him that the CG-1000 still floated.

He wondered, violently, what had occurred. The cruiser was kept just across the inlet, only two or three thousand yards away. Perhaps it had been manned by a crew of the huts. In that case, the three-inch gun would have barked. But Johnny had not heard it. Perhaps the cruiser had overwhelmed the patrol boat without the use of the three-inch gun.

Tight-faced, Johnny waded back through the underbrush. Whatever had happened out there had happened. He could do nothing about it now.

AMBUSH!

JOHNNY TRESCOTT sighted the lighted hut they had first seen. A harsh streak of lightning showed that the clearing about the structure was empty. The door of the hut swung to and fro in the wind.

Johnny pulled back the loading handle of his machine gun. The belt dangled over his shoulder, drooling water from its shiny, brass-studded length. He strode forward, his eyes on the door.

The wind blew the entrance shut in his face. He kicked it open, savagely, commanding the room with his gun. But the structure was empty. An oil lantern burned on the table, half its side blackened by the curling smoke which spewed out of the wick.

The water collected in a pool around his feet. A clock on the sidewall ticked with monotonous regularity. A flash of blue lightning filled the world with glare and sound.

Instinct made Johnny blow out the lamp. An instant later a slug crashed into the clock face, shattering it, stilling it forever. Johnny knew that by ducking his head he had saved his life. That shot had been aimed at his wet, clinging hair.

The door slammed back and forth, prey to the gusts which swooped down from the treetops. The only light in the room came from the single square of window that faced the sea. And that light was the far-off lash of electricity.

Johnny knelt. He found a box and laid the machine gun across it. His movements were unhurried; his face in the darkness was a tight blur. He understood now that this had been a trap. They had him. Probably they were on every side, waiting to rush him. They knew he was armed, but they would rush him anyway. This night, above all others, they would be floating on air with rum, because they thought they needed liquor to drive off the depression of bad weather. Johnny knew they would come, and that they would find him waiting. Heinie and Alicia were dead. They must be by this time. There had been no signal from the sea that all was well.

The waiting was hard. His nerves began to jump under the incessant impact of thunder. When the clearing lighted he thought he could see men moving. But he waited.

From seaward he could hear a motor's throb. Something told him that it would be Georges Coquelin.

The spiteful bark of a revolver sounded outside. The flimsy wood of the wall was pierced. That had been a signal. From every side of the hut, a dozen volleys blasted out. Splinters racketed through the room. Lead smashed itself into screaming slivers against the furnishings.

Johnny ducked his head and hugged the floor. He would not tip his hand yet. Let them think they had gotten him. Let them think that their attempt at murder had been successful.

Johnny felt lightheaded. They couldn't touch him with

those slugs. Let them waste their ammunition. Let them have their fun out there in the rain. He would wait for them. He would wait for their charge. The machine gun was ready to go. Six hundred slugs a minute, traveling with a speed of three thousand feet a second.

The firing stopped for an instant. A voice was bellowing, "Charge him! Get in there and charge him! You won't get him that way, you fools!"

Georges Coquelin!

"Get in there! I've got the woman. Now get *him*!"

Johnny felt as though a bullet had ripped out his heart. Georges had Alicia. Georges had taken her off the 1000. If they didn't charge the hut, Georges would use Alicia as a shield.

Johnny prayed to all the gods that are to let those men charge before Georges thought of using Alicia.

Johnny pressed his face harder against the planking. One hand gripped the machine gun. If they would only charge . . . They'd get him, of course. But not before he had gotten some or all of the others. Wasn't any use to try to escape this, with Ferguson dead.

Abruptly, they charged!

The first was ten feet from the doorway. A massive shape, hurtling forward like a projectile, pistol gripped in a blunt fist.

Johnny sighted and pressed the trips. The man doubled up and slid forward through the mud, carried to the doorstep by his own momentum. Behind him ran others. The line of fire lashed out at them.

Johnny jumped to the door. His arc of fire was widened.

His fingers were as cold and sure as the steel he held and the death he meted out. They still came at him. Their eyes were white spots against the darkness of their faces.

Bullets whined through the hut. Something plucked Johnny's sleeve. A thin trickle coursed down his arm and made his hand slippery. He cursed it. The belt writhed and jerked. The brass empties spewed from the breech and rolled away smoking. Cordite blended with slanting rain.

They were turning now. Turning to escape the death they themselves had tried to mete out. But in turning they stumbled and fell in sodden clots against the mud.

The voice of Georges Coquelin was bellowing at them, but the words were lost in the lash of powder flame and in the rumble of thunder.

The belt ran out. Johnny cocked the machine gun twice before he knew that it was empty. He sank back, clawing at his holstered .45. He expected another rush.

Out front, nothing moved. By the blue glare of lightning he could see them on the ground. He felt a little sick, a little tired.

He heard a whisper of footsteps running away, and remembered that Georges was out there—and that Georges had Alicia.

Georges had his patrol boat out there. He could get away. Johnny laughed, though he knew not why. It was odd to think that Georges would try to get away from him. From Johnny Trescott.

A well of strength as yet unplumbed seeped over his body. He jogged toward the trees, .45 in hand. Lightning showed him the path to the beach and he ran down it, oblivious of the clawing vines, of the slipperiness of the mud. The rain drove at his face and stung him. It probed into his eyes and blinded him. It ran in torrents beneath his clothes and chilled him.

The beach was under his sodden shoes. But it was no longer dark. A searchlight without a body cascaded over him from the center of the cove. It lashed away and came back. It was the CG-1004, Georges' boat.

Johnny saw something else: two hurrying shapes ahead, one hurrying, one holding back. The searchlight shifted again and Johnny cried out.

The first was Georges Coquelin. The other was Alicia. A few feet ahead of them lay a wherry. A few hundred feet across the water lay the patrol boat.

Johnny sprinted forward. He was thirty feet away from them.

"Stop!" Johnny shouted.

Georges brought up a revolver. He aimed carefully and squeezed the trigger.

Johnny dived to the right at the first hammer click. Alicia snatched at Georges' wrist. He threw her away from him. She turned over and over on the sand, to come to rest against the planking of the wharf. She stared up with fascinated eyes.

Johnny held the .45 at the level of his waist. He saw the revolver centering him. In the searchlight's glare he could see Georges' finger coming down on the trigger.

Johnny fired. Sparks ribboned out before him.

A slow look of surprise came across Georges Coquelin's

face. His eyes were round and staring. His hand tried to hold the gun up, but the weapon slipped down, slowly, inch by inch, until it reached his side.

Georges coughed. A trickle of red drooled out from the corner of his thin mouth. Abruptly, he fell on his face, dead.

CHAPTER TWELVE

THE FIRST MATE

JAMES GEORGE FERGUSON was expansive. His pudgy hands rubbed together and his hairless head reflected the light. He was smiling.

"You'll be all right, Trescott," he said.

Johnny looked up from the transom in the main cabin of *The Maid from Hell*. He smiled. Alicia, seated beside him, smoothed his forehead.

"Sure I'll be all right," said Johnny. "But I'll pass out cold again if you don't send Heinie down here."

Heinie's voice from the doorway was jocular. "I'm here. And I can't help but gloat a little bit. My superior officer couldn't have done this job half as well. Now admit it, Johnny!"

"What happened, anyway?" asked Johnny.

"Nothing much. This cruiser met us just as soon as we pulled out of the cove. I put one shot straight through the bridge, and then we opened up with everything we had and—well, they just couldn't take it.

"So when we came aboard, we found Ferguson and all the rest down in the forward hold. Georges' men heard about our escape and they started away just as soon as an obliging radio station broadcasted the news about it. They knew we'd head for here. But we were too fast for them, I guess, and we nailed them. I've got the crew between decks, along with the crew of Georges' patrol boat. They'll keep very nicely, what ho?"

"Righto!" said Johnny. "If you hadn't come into the cove when you did the second time, the CG-1004 would have gotten clean away. That was good work, Heinie."

"You bet it was," Heinie agreed.

Ferguson looked at Johnny and rubbed his hands again. "I suppose, Mr. Trescott, that you'll be leaving the Coast Guard."

"Probably so. It's one great outfit, but after all this, I'm afraid I'd be a curiosity to the rest of the boys. Being a chief petty officer is fine, but I'm afraid they'll try to make an officer out of me after they listen to your weighty testimony."

"And you wouldn't like to be one?" asked Ferguson.

"No. Absolutely not. Besides, I could never make the grade. That takes brains, Ferguson. Real brains."

James George Ferguson smiled. "That's fine. I was afraid you'd want to go on with it, and, of course, I'd be honor-bound to help you, after all you've done for me. Now I can tell you what popped into my mind. I'd like to retain you, Trescott, for about thirty thousand a year."

"To hold down a desk? Nothing doing," said Johnny, flatly.

"No, no, no! You've got me all wrong, Trescott. All wrong. Do you think I would offer you anything like that, after all you've done for me?

"You see," continued Ferguson, "I happen to own a fleet of small trading vessels down in South America. I have a lot of trouble down there with piracy of sorts and the natives up the rivers, and I thought if you—"

"No!" said Johnny.

"But—but my Lord, man—!"

"Not unless you hire a good mate for me."

"Well," said Ferguson, "I guess—" He smiled in sudden comprehension.

"Young man," he said, "I think, by the way that young lady is looking at you, that you've already hired your mate—for life."

"That's right," said Johnny, grinning. "That's what I meant. Without Alicia, the firm of Johnny and Company would be nothing."

"Okay," said Alicia. "I accept both jobs. And if you . . ."

The engines were throbbing down below, and the spent wind of the storm was helping take them north. Ahead, the horizon stretched out, pearl clear with the coming sun. A breath of fresh, cool air fanned through the open port and blessed them.

STORY PREVIEW

STORY PREVIEW

NOW that you've just ventured through one of the captivating tales in the Stories from the Golden Age collection by L. Ron Hubbard, turn the page and enjoy a preview of *False Cargo*. Join Brent Calloway, hired by an insurance firm to board a cargo vessel undercover and make sure it makes its way to San Diego in one piece. Once the voyage is underway, Calloway finds fraud, a pattern of organized scuttlings, and the true fate of another vessel captained by an old friend. When Calloway's true identity is revealed, he must fight for his life—and the real danger begins.

FALSE CARGO

SPIKE O'BRIEN'S bull bellow was deceptively hearty, gratingly cheerful. With one foot planted on the brass rail before the Honolulu bar, with a slopping glass of liquor tottering before his gross face, he roared, "Come on up here, every one of you sons! You're goin' to drink to the toughest man that ever sailed the Pacific. Snap into it, me buckos!"

A Kanaka-Chinese breed moved cautiously away, his black eyes bright with fear of the swaying bulk beside him. Spike O'Brien caught the movement out of the corner of his bloodshot eye. With a jerk of his thick wrist he sent both glass and liquor hurtling into the half-caste's face.

With a scream, the small yellow man clawed at his eyes and stumbled away. Blood was running down into his mouth from a cut jaw.

O'Brien laughed. The sound shattered even the noisy turmoil of the Honolulu dive. Men stopped and stared.

"Come up here, every one of you!" snarled O'Brien with a leer. "Come up here and drink to the toughest man on the Pacific. Spike O'Brien. S-P-I-K-E, Spike. O-B-R-I-E-N, O'Brien. The man who killed Shen Su. The guy who whipped the governor of Borneo. I'll take on any two of you—any three of you. I'll fight the whole damned bunch of you with both hands tied. Come on up here and *drink*!"

The fat barkeep stopped dispensing coolyhow and swabbed his greasy forehead. His eyes were pleading with someone, anyone, to do something about this. Men were stumbling up the steps that led to the dock street, deserting the place, trading its external and internal warmth for Honolulu's wet fog.

O'Brien turned around and swept his apparently drink-glazed eyes across the room and its remaining occupants. He was a tremendous bulk of a man, clad in black pea jacket, white-topped cap. His coat swung open and light fell on the brass buckle against his waist.

O'Brien's eyes rested on the far side of the room, went away and came back again. His mouth twitched with annoyance.

A white man sat there, quietly spinning a small glass between thumb and index finger. His hands were narrow and tapering as are those of an artist. His face was the face of a saint. His shoulders were of awesome dimensions, even though he was noticeably slender. O'Brien's annoyed glance rested on the quiet face, seeing only the fine features of a gentleman, completely missing the small light which danced far back in the metallic gray eyes. The face might be that of a saint, but the eyes did not match.

O'Brien did not like either face or fingers. He had ordered all up to the bar for a drink and this man had not answered the call.

"Hey, you!" barked O'Brien. "Come up here, unnerstand? You're going to have a drink with me whether *you* like it or not, see?"

The face showed very little interest. The small sparkling glass went round and round between the slim fingers.

O'Brien lurched away from the bar. The lurch was exaggerated. It took more than a dozen drinks to make Spike O'Brien that drunk. His eyes were suddenly cold, shining with an animal intelligence.

"You'll come up to this bar or I'll drag you up!" promised O'Brien, jolting against the table, spilling the other's glass.

"You annoy me, Mr. O'Brien. And I don't like your face. Get out of here before I change my mind about dirtying my hands on you." In spite of the import of the words, the quiet face did not change or show the slightest interest or emotion. The small lights in the eyes were flaring up steadily.

"You . . . you talk that way to Spike O'Brien?" O'Brien was plainly dumbfounded, aghast. He slapped his hairy hands down on the scarred top of the table and thrust his jaw close to the other's face. "Maybe—" said O'Brien, "maybe you don't know who I am."

"Probably not."

"Well, I'm Spike O'Brien, that's who I am. I'm the man Ring and Talbot brought all the way from China to do a job for 'em. I'm tough, get me? I'd just as soon *kill* you as look at you."

"Please take your face away," said the other mildly. "Your breath is bad. Haven't you any friends to tell you?"

O'Brien rocked back on his heels. His red-rimmed eyes focused on the other's face. His coarse lips moved soundlessly for a moment and then words exploded from them.

"Say, I know you . . . you're Brent Calloway!" he yowled.

The other nodded. "Yes . . . Brent Calloway. What were you saying a moment ago about being the toughest man

101

on the China coast? That scar on your jaw looks familiar, O'Brien."

The scarred jaw was jutting. O'Brien rocked on his heels, though he was plainly cold sober. He studied the other's position. A man sitting down makes a good target—he cannot dodge.

O'Brien's hand snapped to his belt. A short Derringer, smaller than the palm of his hand, capable of throwing two .45 slugs in less than two seconds, gleamed an instant under the hanging lantern.

Brent Calloway's fist disappeared under the lapel of his jacket. Flame blasted out from the table's edge. A second ribbon of sparks leaped up to scorch O'Brien's face.

The Derringer dropped with a clatter. A widening stare of surprise spread across O'Brien's coarse, flat features. His hands groped for the table edge. Abruptly he dropped, as though something had cut the string that held him up. The stubby fingers closed twice, and then O'Brien lay still.

Brent Calloway shoved the automatic back into his shoulder holster and glanced up at the entrance. Police might arrive any moment. All men had vanished from the basement dive.

Calloway stood for a moment staring down at the loosely sprawled form. A grimace of distaste passed across his face. Bending over, he thrust a hand into O'Brien's shirt and brought forth a packet of papers wrapped in a strip of oilcloth. Pocketing these, he walked steadily to the door and mounted the steps.

The fog closed in behind him.

O'Brien twisted about with a pain-racked grunt, finding just enough energy to shake his fist at the door and mutter, "This time you won't get away with it—not this time, Brent Calloway!"

To find out more about *False Cargo* and how you can obtain your copy, go to www.goldenagestories.com.

GLOSSARY

STORIES FROM THE GOLDEN AGE *reflect the words and expressions used in the 1930s and 1940s, adding unique flavor and authenticity to the tales. While a character's speech may often reflect regional origins, it also can convey attitudes common in the day. So that readers can better grasp such cultural and historical terms, uncommon words or expressions of the era, the following glossary has been provided.*

---

abeam: off to the side of a ship, especially at a right angle to the middle of the ship's length.

after hatch: an opening in a boat's deck, toward the stern, which is fitted with a watertight cover.

aileron: a hinged flap on the trailing edge of an aircraft wing, used to control banking movements.

anchorage: that portion of a harbor, or area outside a harbor, suitable for anchoring, or in which ships are permitted to anchor.

anvil chorus: in reference to a piece of music, "The Troubadour," by Italian composer Giuseppe Verdi (1813–1901), that depicts Spanish gypsies striking their anvils at dawn and singing the praises of hard work, good wine and their gypsy women.

astern: in a position behind a specified vessel.

banshee: (Irish legend) a female spirit whose wailing warns of a death in a house.

barratry: fraud by a master or crew at the expense of the owners of the ship or its cargo.

binnacle: a built-in housing for a ship's compass.

Borneo: the third largest island in the world, located in southeastern Asia, in the western Pacific Ocean to the north of the Java Sea.

bosun: a ship's officer in charge of supervision and maintenance of the ship and its equipment.

bucko: young fellow; chap; young companion.

bulwark: a solid wall enclosing the perimeter of a weather or main deck for the protection of persons or objects on deck.

Cajun: a Louisianan descended from French-speaking immigrants from Acadia, a former French colony in Canada.

cameo: a small piece of sculpture on a stone or shell having two layers of different colors, the figure being cut in relief in one layer, and another serving as background.

chronometer: an instrument for measuring time accurately in spite of motion or varying conditions.

collar ad: collar and shirt advertisements by J. C. Leyendecker (1874–1951), an illustrator and entrepreneur who defined an era of fashion in the early twentieth century. He painted strong, athletic men and created long-running characters for the Arrow collar man ads (Arrow was a brand of shirt), as well as many others.

Colt: an automatic pistol manufactured by the Colt Firearms Company, founded in 1847 by Samuel Colt (1814–1862) who revolutionized the firearms industry with his inventions.

coolyhow: a drink.

cordite: a family of smokeless propellants, developed and produced in the United Kingdom from the late nineteenth century to replace gunpowder as a military propellant for large weapons, such as tank guns, artillery and naval guns. Cordite is now obsolete and no longer produced.

Cyclops: USS *Cyclops* (1910–1918), a Navy ship that was specially designed to keep a mobile battle fleet supplied with fuel and carried coal to facilitate the US Navy's wartime operations. In early March 1918, while returning from Brazil, the *Cyclops* disappeared with all hands. Her wreck has never been found and the cause of her loss remains unknown.

davits: any of various cranelike devices, used singly or in pairs, for supporting, raising and lowering boats, anchors and cargo over a hatchway or side of a ship.

dead to rights: in the very act of committing a crime, offense or mistake; red-handed.

Derringer: a pocket-sized, short-barreled, large-caliber pistol. Named for the US gunsmith Henry Deringer (1786–1868), who designed it.

drop on, got the: to have a distinct advantage over someone, especially through early or quick action. From the mid-1800s it originally alluded to pointing one's gun at someone before he pointed his at you.

Errol Island: formerly one of the Chandeleur Islands, a chain of islands located east of New Orleans in the Gulf of Mexico. By 1951, Errol Island was completely submerged and it no longer exists.

foil: a light, slender sword with a blunted point, used in the art or practice of fencing.

gangway: a narrow, movable platform or ramp forming a bridge by which to board or leave a ship.

G-men: government men; agents of the Federal Bureau of Investigation.

gunwale: the upper edge of the side of a boat. Originally a gunwale was a platform where guns were mounted, and was designed to accommodate the additional stresses imposed by the artillery being used.

half-caste: a person of mixed racial descent.

hawse pipes: iron or steel pipes in the stem or bow of a vessel, through which anchor cables pass.

hein?: (French) eh?

hull: to pierce the hull of a ship, especially below the water line.

hydrographic map: a nautical map showing depths of water, nature of bottom, contours of bottom and coastline, and tides and currents in a given sea or sea and land area.

Jacob's ladder: a hanging ladder having ropes or chains supporting wooden or metal rungs or steps.

Jupiter Pluv: (Roman mythology) Jupiter Pluvius, Roman king of the gods, also known as the Rain-giver.

Kanaka: a native Hawaiian.

key: a hand-operated device used to transmit Morse code messages.

knee-high to a seagull: variation of "knee-high to a grasshopper"; quite young.

knot: a unit of speed, equal to one nautical mile, or about 1.15 miles, per hour.

lam: to escape or run away, especially from the law.

lanyard: a cord attached to a cannon's trigger mechanism, which when pulled, fires the cannon.

lay to: 1. turn into the wind to stop or gain control in heavy weather. A power vessel would turn into the seas and apply just enough power to maintain position. 2. to attack vigorously.

lit: intoxicated.

lockjaw: a nervous system disease brought on by bacteria that cause muscles to seize up and may cause death by suffocation.

log: patent log; a propeller drawn through the water that operates a meter on the boat registering the speed and distance sailed.

monkey fist: a ball-like knot used as an ornament or as a throwing weight at the end of a line.

navy: a body or fleet of ships with their crews.

one-pound gun or **one-pounder:** a gun firing a one-pound shot or shell. It looks somewhat like a miniature cannon.

pink tea: formal tea, reception or other social gathering usually attended by politicians, military officials and the like.

plugged *centavo:* a worthless coin. A plugged coin was counterfeit or had a plug of metal removed from the center. *Centavo* is Spanish for a cent or penny.

points: a point is 11.25 degrees on a compass, thus two points would be 22.50 degrees.

reduction gear: a set of gears in an engine used to reduce output speed relative to that of the engine while providing greater turning power.

rigger: a mechanic skilled in the assembly, adjustment and alignment of aircraft control surfaces, wings and the like.

rummies: rumrunners; people or ships engaged in bringing prohibited liquor ashore or across a border.

Scheherazade: the female narrator of *The Arabian Nights,* who during one thousand and one adventurous nights saved her life by entertaining her husband, the king, with stories.

scow: an old or clumsy boat; hulk; tub.

scuppers: gutters along the edge of the deck that drain into openings in the side of a ship that allow water to run off.

ship a sea: when the sea breaks into the ship and is received on board.

sou'wester: a waterproof hat with a wide brim that widens in the back to protect the neck in stormy weather, worn especially by seamen.

spars: strong poles, especially those used as masts to support the sails on ships.

SS: steamship.

stanchion: an upright bar, post or frame forming a support or barrier.

struts: supports for a structure such as an aircraft wing, roof or bridge.

tin can: 1. a ship's engines. 2. a destroyer; a small fast warship. The nickname arose because in World Wars I and II, the hull plating of this type of ship was so thin the sailors claimed they were made from tin cans. In fact, a .45-caliber pistol bullet would penetrate it. Modern destroyers have much thicker hull plating, but the nickname persists.

transom: transom seat; a kind of bench seat, usually with a locker or drawers underneath.

wherry: a light rowboat for use transporting goods and passengers in inland waters and harbors.

L. Ron Hubbard
in the Golden Age
of Pulp Fiction

*In writing an adventure story
a writer has to know that he is adventuring
for a lot of people who cannot.
The writer has to take them here and there
about the globe and show them
excitement and love and realism.
As long as that writer is living the part of an
adventurer when he is hammering
the keys, he is succeeding with his story.*

*Adventuring is a state of mind.
If you adventure through life, you have a
good chance to be a success on paper.*

*Adventure doesn't mean globe-trotting,
exactly, and it doesn't mean great deeds.
Adventuring is like art.
You have to live it to make it real.*

—*L. RON HUBBARD*

L. Ron Hubbard
and American
Pulp Fiction

B ORN March 13, 1911, L. Ron Hubbard lived a life at least as expansive as the stories with which he enthralled a hundred million readers through a fifty-year career.

Originally hailing from Tilden, Nebraska, he spent his formative years in a classically rugged Montana, replete with the cowpunchers, lawmen and desperadoes who would later people his Wild West adventures. And lest anyone imagine those adventures were drawn from vicarious experience, he was not only breaking broncs at a tender age, he was also among the few whites ever admitted into Blackfoot society as a bona fide blood brother. While if only to round out an otherwise rough and tumble youth, his mother was that rarity of her time—a thoroughly educated woman—who introduced her son to the classics of Occidental literature even before his seventh birthday.

But as any dedicated L. Ron Hubbard reader will attest, his world extended far beyond Montana. In point of fact, and as the son of a United States naval officer, by the age of eighteen he had traveled over a quarter of a million miles. Included therein were three Pacific crossings to a then still mysterious Asia, where he ran with the likes of Her British Majesty's agent-in-place

L. Ron Hubbard, left, at Congressional Airport, Washington, DC, 1931, with members of George Washington University flying club.

for North China, and the last in the line of Royal Magicians from the court of Kublai Khan. For the record, L. Ron Hubbard was also among the first Westerners to gain admittance to forbidden Tibetan monasteries below Manchuria, and his photographs of China's Great Wall long graced American geography texts.

Upon his return to the United States and a hasty completion of his interrupted high school education, the young Ron Hubbard entered George Washington University. There, as fans of his aerial adventures may have heard, he earned his wings as a pioneering barnstormer at the dawn of American aviation. He also earned a place in free-flight record books for the longest sustained flight above Chicago. Moreover, as a roving reporter for *Sportsman Pilot* (featuring his first professionally penned articles), he further helped inspire a generation of pilots who would take America to world airpower.

Immediately beyond his sophomore year, Ron embarked on the first of his famed ethnological expeditions, initially to then untrammeled Caribbean shores (descriptions of which would later fill a whole series of West Indies mystery-thrillers). That the Puerto Rican interior would also figure into the future of Ron Hubbard stories was likewise no accident. For in addition to cultural studies of the island, a 1932–33

LRH expedition is rightly remembered as conducting the first complete mineralogical survey of a Puerto Rico under United States jurisdiction.

There was many another adventure along this vein: As a lifetime member of the famed Explorers Club, L. Ron Hubbard charted North Pacific waters with the first shipboard radio direction finder, and so pioneered a long-range navigation system universally employed until the late twentieth century. While not to put too fine an edge on it, he also held a rare Master Mariner's license to pilot any vessel, of any tonnage in any ocean.

Yet lest we stray too far afield, there is an LRH note at this juncture in his saga, and it reads in part:

"I started out writing for the pulps, writing the best I knew, writing for every mag on the stands, slanting as well as I could."

To which one might add: His earliest submissions date from the summer of 1934, and included tales drawn from true-to-life Asian adventures, with characters roughly modeled on British/American intelligence operatives he had known in Shanghai. His early Westerns were similarly peppered with details drawn from personal

Capt. L. Ron Hubbard in Ketchikan, Alaska, 1940, on his Alaskan Radio Experimental Expedition, the first of three voyages conducted under the Explorers Club flag.

experience. Although therein lay a first hard lesson from the often cruel world of the pulps. His first Westerns were soundly rejected as lacking the authenticity of a Max Brand yarn (a particularly frustrating comment given L. Ron Hubbard's Westerns came straight from his Montana homeland, while Max Brand was a mediocre New York poet named Frederick Schiller Faust, who turned out implausible six-shooter tales from the terrace of an Italian villa).

Nevertheless, and needless to say, L. Ron Hubbard persevered and soon earned a reputation as among the most publishable names in pulp fiction, with a ninety percent placement rate of first-draft manuscripts. He was also among the most prolific, averaging between seventy and a hundred thousand words a month. Hence the rumors that L. Ron Hubbard had redesigned a typewriter for faster keyboard action and pounded out manuscripts on a continuous roll of butcher paper to save the precious seconds it took to insert a single sheet of paper into manual typewriters of the day.

That all L. Ron Hubbard stories did not run beneath said byline is yet another aspect of pulp fiction lore. That is, as publishers periodically rejected manuscripts from top-drawer authors if only to avoid paying top dollar, L. Ron Hubbard and company just as frequently replied with submissions under various pseudonyms. In Ron's case, the

A MAN OF MANY NAMES

Between 1934 and 1950, L. Ron Hubbard authored more than fifteen million words of fiction in more than two hundred classic publications. To supply his fans and editors with stories across an array of genres and pulp titles, he adopted fifteen pseudonyms in addition to his already renowned L. Ron Hubbard byline.

*Winchester Remington Colt
Lt. Jonathan Daly
Capt. Charles Gordon
Capt. L. Ron Hubbard
Bernard Hubbel
Michael Keith
Rene Lafayette
Legionnaire 148
Legionnaire 14830
Ken Martin
Scott Morgan
Lt. Scott Morgan
Kurt von Rachen
Barry Randolph
Capt. Humbert Reynolds*

list included: Rene Lafayette, Captain Charles Gordon, Lt. Scott Morgan and the notorious Kurt von Rachen—supposedly on the lam for a murder rap, while hammering out two-fisted prose in Argentina. The point: While L. Ron Hubbard as Ken Martin spun stories of Southeast Asian intrigue, LRH as Barry Randolph authored tales of romance on the Western range—which, stretching between a dozen genres is how he came to stand among the two hundred elite authors providing close to a million tales through the glory days of American Pulp Fiction.

L. Ron Hubbard, circa 1930, at the outset of a literary career that would finally span half a century.

In evidence of exactly that, by 1936 L. Ron Hubbard was literally leading pulp fiction's elite as president of New York's American Fiction Guild. Members included a veritable pulp hall of fame: Lester "Doc Savage" Dent, Walter "The Shadow" Gibson, and the legendary Dashiell Hammett—to cite but a few.

Also in evidence of just where L. Ron Hubbard stood within his first two years on the American pulp circuit: By the spring of 1937, he was ensconced in Hollywood, adopting a Caribbean thriller for Columbia Pictures, remembered today as *The Secret of Treasure Island*. Comprising fifteen thirty-minute episodes, the L. Ron Hubbard screenplay led to the most profitable matinée serial in Hollywood history. In accord with Hollywood culture, he was thereafter continually called upon

The 1937 Secret of Treasure Island, *a fifteen-episode serial adapted for the screen by L. Ron Hubbard from his novel,* Murder at Pirate Castle.

to rewrite/doctor scripts—most famously for long-time friend and fellow adventurer Clark Gable.

In the interim—and herein lies another distinctive chapter of the L. Ron Hubbard story—he continually worked to open Pulp Kingdom gates to up-and-coming authors. Or, for that matter, anyone who wished to write. It was a fairly unconventional stance, as markets were already thin and competition razor sharp. But the fact remains, it was an L. Ron Hubbard hallmark that he vehemently lobbied on behalf of young authors—regularly supplying instructional articles to trade journals, guest-lecturing to short story classes at George Washington University and Harvard, and even founding his own creative writing competition. It was established in 1940, dubbed the Golden Pen, and guaranteed winners both New York representation and publication in *Argosy*.

But it was John W. Campbell Jr.'s *Astounding Science Fiction* that finally proved the most memorable LRH vehicle. While every fan of L. Ron Hubbard's galactic epics undoubtedly knows the story, it nonetheless bears repeating: By late 1938, the pulp publishing magnate of Street & Smith was determined to revamp *Astounding Science Fiction* for broader readership. In particular, senior editorial director F. Orlin Tremaine called for stories with a stronger *human element*. When acting editor John W. Campbell balked, preferring his spaceship-driven tales, Tremaine enlisted Hubbard. Hubbard, in turn, replied with the genre's first truly *character-driven* works, wherein heroes are pitted not against bug-eyed monsters but the mystery and majesty of deep space itself—and thus was launched the Golden Age of Science Fiction.

The names alone are enough to quicken the pulse of any science fiction aficionado, including LRH friend and protégé, Robert Heinlein, Isaac Asimov, A. E. van Vogt and Ray Bradbury. Moreover, when coupled with LRH stories of fantasy, we further come to what's rightly been described as the foundation of every modern tale of horror: L. Ron Hubbard's immortal *Fear*. It was rightly proclaimed by Stephen King as one of the very few works to genuinely warrant that overworked term "classic"—as in: *"This is a classic tale of creeping, surreal menace and horror. . . . This is one of the really, really good ones."*

To accommodate the greater body of L. Ron Hubbard fantasies, Street & Smith inaugurated *Unknown*—a classic pulp if there ever was one, and wherein readers were soon thrilling to the likes of *Typewriter in the Sky* and *Slaves of Sleep* of which Frederik Pohl would declare: *"There are bits and pieces from Ron's work that became part of the language in ways that very few other writers managed."*

L. Ron Hubbard, 1948, among fellow science fiction luminaries at the World Science Fiction Convention in Toronto.

And, indeed, at J. W. Campbell Jr.'s insistence, Ron was regularly drawing on themes from the Arabian Nights and so introducing readers to a world of genies, jinn, Aladdin and Sinbad—all of which, of course, continue to float through cultural mythology to this day.

At least as influential in terms of post-apocalypse stories was L. Ron Hubbard's 1940 *Final Blackout*. Generally acclaimed as the finest anti-war novel of the decade and among the ten best works of the genre ever authored—here, too, was a tale that would live on in ways few other writers imagined.

Portland, Oregon, 1943; L. Ron Hubbard, captain of the US Navy subchaser PC 815.

Hence, the later Robert Heinlein verdict: "Final Blackout *is as perfect a piece of science fiction as has ever been written.*"

Like many another who both lived and wrote American pulp adventure, the war proved a tragic end to Ron's sojourn in the pulps. He served with distinction in four theaters and was highly decorated for commanding corvettes in the North Pacific. He was also grievously wounded in combat, lost many a close friend and colleague and thus resolved to say farewell to pulp fiction and devote himself to what it had supported these many years—namely, his serious research.

But in no way was the LRH literary saga at an end, for as he wrote some thirty years later, in 1980:

"Recently there came a period when I had little to do. This was novel in a life so crammed with busy years, and I decided to amuse myself by writing a novel that was pure *science fiction."*

That work was *Battlefield Earth: A Saga of the Year 3000*. It was an immediate *New York Times* bestseller and, in fact, the first international science fiction blockbuster in decades. It was not, however, L. Ron Hubbard's magnum opus, as that distinction is generally reserved for his next and final work: The 1.2 million word *Mission Earth*.

> **Final Blackout**
> *is as perfect
> a piece of
> science fiction
> as has ever
> been written.*
>
> **—Robert Heinlein**

How he managed those 1.2 million words in just over twelve months is yet another piece of the L. Ron Hubbard legend. But the fact remains, he did indeed author a ten-volume *dekalogy* that lives in publishing history for the fact that each and every volume of the series was also a *New York Times* bestseller.

Moreover, as subsequent generations discovered L. Ron Hubbard through republished works and novelizations of his screenplays, the mere fact of his name on a cover signaled an international bestseller. . . . Until, to date, sales of his works exceed hundreds of millions, and he otherwise remains among the most enduring and widely read authors in literary history. Although as a final word on the tales of L. Ron Hubbard, perhaps it's enough to simply reiterate what editors told readers in the glory days of American Pulp Fiction:

He writes the way he does, brothers, because he's been there, seen it and done it!

THE STORIES FROM THE GOLDEN AGE

Your ticket to adventure starts here with the Stories from
the Golden Age collection by master storyteller L. Ron Hubbard.
These gripping tales are set in a kaleidoscope of exotic locales and brim
with fascinating characters, including some of the
most vile villains, dangerous dames and brazen heroes
you'll ever get to meet.

The entire collection of over one hundred and fifty stories is being
released in a series of eighty books and audiobooks.
For an up-to-date listing of available titles,
go to www.goldenagestories.com.

AIR ADVENTURE

Arctic Wings	*Man-Killers of the Air*
The Battling Pilot	*On Blazing Wings*
Boomerang Bomber	*Red Death Over China*
The Crate Killer	*Sabotage in the Sky*
The Dive Bomber	*Sky Birds Dare!*
Forbidden Gold	*The Sky-Crasher*
Hurtling Wings	*Trouble on His Wings*
The Lieutenant Takes the Sky	*Wings Over Ethiopia*

FAR-FLUNG ADVENTURE

SEA ADVENTURE

TALES FROM THE ORIENT

MYSTERY

FANTASY

Borrowed Glory	*If I Were You*
The Crossroads	*The Last Drop*
Danger in the Dark	*The Room*
The Devil's Rescue	*The Tramp*
He Didn't Like Cats	

SCIENCE FICTION

The Automagic Horse	*A Matter of Matter*
Battle of Wizards	*The Obsolete Weapon*
Battling Bolto	*One Was Stubborn*
The Beast	*The Planet Makers*
Beyond All Weapons	*The Professor Was a Thief*
A Can of Vacuum	*The Slaver*
The Conroy Diary	*Space Can*
The Dangerous Dimension	*Strain*
Final Enemy	*Tough Old Man*
The Great Secret	*240,000 Miles Straight Up*
Greed	*When Shadows Fall*
The Invaders	

WESTERN

Your Next Ticket to Adventure

Capture all of the
Pulse-Pounding Action!

Hired by Lloyd's insurance company to ensure the safe voyage
of the vessel *Barclay* from Hawaii to San Diego, skipper Brent
Calloway finds himself caught in an illegal scheme to scuttle
the ship in order to collect money. At the center of the plot is
none other than Spike O'Brien, known throughout
the Pacific as a ruthless killer.

Compounding Calloway's troubles on deck, he sees that O'Brien
also has lecherous claws for Dorothy, a passenger and the sister
of one of Brent's best friends. When the *Barclay* heads for
the rocks and threatens to run aground, Brent makes a
discovery which turns everything upside down.

Get
False Cargo

PAPERBACK OR AUDIOBOOK: **$9.95** EACH
Free Shipping & Handling for Book Club Members
CALL TOLL-FREE: 1-877-8GALAXY (1-877-842-5299)
OR GO ONLINE TO **www.goldenagestories.com**

Galaxy Press, 7051 Hollywood Blvd., Suite 200, Hollywood, CA 90028

JOIN THE PULP REVIVAL
America in the 1930s and 40s

Pulp fiction was in its heyday and 30 million readers were regularly riveted by the larger-than-life tales of master storyteller L. Ron Hubbard. For this was pulp fiction's golden age, when the writing was raw and every page packed a walloping punch.

That magic can now be yours. An evocative world of nefarious villains, exotic intrigues, courageous heroes and heroines—a world that today's cinema has barely tapped for tales of adventure and swashbucklers.

Enroll today in the Stories from the Golden Age Club and begin receiving your monthly feature edition selected from more than 150 stories in the collection.

You may choose to enjoy them as either a paperback or audiobook for the special membership price of $9.95 each month along with FREE shipping and handling.

CALL TOLL-FREE: **1-877-8GALAXY**
(1-877-842-5299) OR GO ONLINE TO
www.goldenagestories.com
AND BECOME PART OF THE PULP REVIVAL!

Prices are set in US dollars only. For non-US residents, please call
1-323-466-7815 for pricing information. Free shipping available for US residents only.

Galaxy Press, 7051 Hollywood Blvd., Suite 200, Hollywood, CA 90028